Undiscovered

Anna Hackett

Undiscovered

Published by Anna Hackett
Copyright 2016 by Anna Hackett
Cover by Melody Simmons of eBookindiecovers
Edits by Tanya Saari

ISBN (eBook): 978-0-9945572-4-7
ISBN (paperback): 978-0-9945572-6-1

What readers are saying about Anna's Science
Fiction Romance

At Star's End – One of Library Journal's Best
E-Original Romances for 2014

Return to Dark Earth – One of Library Journal's
Best E-Original Books for 2015 and two-time SFR
Galaxy Awards winner

The Phoenix Adventures – SFR Galaxy Award
Winner for Most Fun New Series and "Why Isn't
This a Movie?" Series

Beneath a Trojan Moon – SFR Galaxy Award
Winner and RWAus Ella Award Winner

Hell Squad – Amazon Bestselling Sci-fi Romance
Series and SFR Galaxy Award Winner

"Like Indiana Jones meets Star Wars. A treasure
hunt with a steamy romance." – SFF Dragon,
review of *Among Galactic Ruins*

"Fun, action-packed read that I thoroughly enjoyed.
The romance was steamy, there's a whole heap of
supporting characters I can't wait to get to know
better and there's enough archeology and history to
satisfy my inner geek." – Book Gannet Reviews
review of *Undiscovered*

"Strap in, enjoy the heat of romance and the daring of this group of space travellers!" – Di, Top 500 Amazon Reviewer, review of *At Star's End*

Don't miss out! For updates about new releases, action romance info, free books, and other fun stuff, sign up for my VIP mailing list and get your *free box set* containing three action-packed romances.

Visit here to get started:

www.annahackettbooks.com

Chapter One

She was hot, dusty, and she'd never felt better.

Dr. Layne Rush walked across her dig, her boots sinking into the hot Egyptian sand. Ahead, she saw her team of archeologists and students kneeling over the new section of the dig, dusting sand away with brushes and small spades, methodically uncovering a recently discovered burial ground.

To her left, the yawning hole in the ground where they'd started the dig was like a large mouth, ringed on one side by a wooden scaffold.

In there, below the sands, was a fantastic tomb, and Layne was only beginning to unravel its secrets.

She paused and drew in a breath of warm desert air. To the east lay the Nile, the lifeblood of Egypt. She swiveled and watched the red-orange orb of the sun sinking into the Western Desert sands. All around, the dunes glowed. It made her think of gold.

Excitement was a hit to her bloodstream. Only days ago, they'd discovered some stunning golden artifacts down in the excavation. She'd found the first one—a small ushabti funerary figurine that would have been placed there to serve the tomb's as-yet-unknown occupant in the afterlife. After that, her team had discovered jewelry, a golden scarab, and a small amulet of a dog-like animal.

Stars started appearing in the sky, like tiny pinpricks of light through velvet. She breathed in again. The most exciting thing was the strange inscriptions carved into the dog amulet.

They had mentioned Zerzura.

Oh, Layne really wanted to believe Zerzura existed—a fabulous lost oasis in the desert, filled with treasure. She smiled as she watched the night darkness shroud the dunes. Her parents had read her bedtime stories of Zerzura as a child.

Thoughts of her parents, and the hard punch of grief that followed, made Layne's smile disappear. Unfortunately, life had taught her that fairytales didn't exist.

She shook off the melancholy. She'd made a life for herself, a career, and spent most of her time off on adventures on remote dig sites. She'd held treasures in her hands. She shared her love of history with anyone who'd listen. She hoped that if her mom and dad were still alive, they'd be proud of what she'd achieved.

Layne made her way toward the large square tents set up for dealing with the artifacts. One was for storage and one for study.

"Hey, Dr. Rush."

Layne spotted her assistant, Piper Ross, trudging up the dune toward her. The young woman was smart, opinionated, and not afraid to speak her mind. Her dark hair was cut short, the tips colored purple.

"Hi, Piper."

The young woman grinned. "Give you a whip and you'd look like something out of a movie." Piper swept a palm through the air. "Dr. Rush, dashing female adventurer."

Layne rolled her eyes. "Don't start. I still haven't lived down that last interview I did." What Layne had thought was a serious article on archeology had morphed into a story that turned her into a damned movie character. They'd even Photoshopped a whip in her hand and a hat on her head. "How's that new eastern quadrant coming along?"

"Excellent." Piper stopped, swiping her arm across her sweaty forehead. "I've got it all documented and photographed, and the tape laid out. We're ready to start digging tomorrow morning."

"Well done." Layne was hoping the new area would yield some excellent finds.

"Well, I *am* insanely good at my job—that's why you hired me, remember?" Piper grinned.

Layne tapped her chin. "Was that it? I thought it was because you kept me in a constant supply of Diet Coke and chocolate."

Piper snorted. "Here they call it Coke Light, remember?"

Layne screwed up her nose. "I remember. The damn stuff doesn't taste the same."

"Yes, you really have to suffer out here on these remote digs."

"Can the sarcasm, Ross. Or I might forget why I keep you around."

Piper laughed. "A few of us are heading into Dakhla for the evening. Want to come?"

Dakhla Oasis was a two-hour drive north-east of the dig site. A group of communities, including the main town of Mut, were centered on the oasis. It was also where most of their local workers came from, and where they got their supplies.

Layne shook her head. "No, but thanks for the offer. I want to spend a bit more time on the artifacts we found, and take another look at the tomb plans. The main burial chamber and sarcophagus have to be in there somewhere."

"Unless grave robbers got to it," Piper suggested.

Layne shook her head. "When that local boy discovered this place it was clearly undisturbed." In between the discovery that had made headlines and her university being awarded the right to dig, the Egyptian Ministry of Antiquities had kept tight security on the place. She knew the Ministry would have preferred to run the dig themselves, but they just didn't have the funding to run every dig in the country. "I'm going to find out who's buried here, Piper."

The younger woman shook her head. "Well, just remember, all work and no play makes Dr. Rush very boring and in need of getting laid."

Layne rolled her eyes. "I'll worry about my personal life, thanks for your concern."

Piper stuck her hand on her hip. "You haven't dated since Dr. Stevens."

Ugh. Just hearing her colleague's name made Layne's stomach turn over. Dr. Evan Stevens had been a colossal mistake. He was tall and handsome, in a clean-cut way that suited his academic career as a professor of the Classics and History.

He'd been nice, intelligent. They'd liked the same restaurants. The sex hadn't been stellar, but it was fine. Layne had honestly thought he was someone she could come to love. More than anything, Layne wanted it all—a career, to travel, a husband who loved her, and most importantly, a family of her own. She wanted the love she remembered her parents sharing. She wanted the career they'd only dreamed of for her.

Maybe that had blinded her to the fact that Evan was an asshole hiding in an expensive suit.

Layne waved a hand dismissively. "I've told you before, I don't want to hear that man's name."

"I know you guys had a bad breakup..."

Ha. Piper didn't know half of it. Evan had stolen some of Layne's research and passed it off as his own. And he'd had the gall to tell her she was bad in bed. Moron.

"Look, go," Layne said. "Head into the oasis, soak in the springs, relax. You've got a lot of work to do tomorrow in the hot sun."

Piper groaned. "Don't remind me."

But Layne could see the twinkle of excitement in the young woman's eye. Layne saw it in her own every day. Being on a dig was always like that. Uncovering a piece of history...she could never truly describe how it made her feel. To touch something that someone had made, used, and cherished thousands of years ago. To uncover its secrets and try to piece together where it fit into the story of the world. To see what they could learn from it that might help them understand more about humanity.

She found it endlessly fascinating. Best job in the world.

After waving Piper off, Layne headed to the storage tent. The canvas door was still rolled up and secured at the top. As she stepped inside, the temperature dropped a little. Now that the sun had set, the temperature would drop even more. Nights in the desert, even in spring, could be chilly. She'd need to get to the portable shower they had set up and rinse off before it got too cold.

She'd lost count of the number of digs she'd been on. In the jungle, in the desert, under cities, by the ocean. She didn't care where they were, she just loved the challenge and thrill of uncovering the past.

Layne flicked on the battery-powered lantern hanging on the side of the tent. Makeshift shelves lined the space. Most were bare, waiting for the treasures they had yet to discover. But the first shelf was lined with shards of pottery, faience amulets, and stone carvings. But it was the locked box at the base of the shelf she was most interested in.

She quickly dialed in the code on the tumbler-style lock and lifted the lid.

God. She stroked the ushabti reverently, its gold

surface glowing in the lantern-light. Her parents would have loved to have seen this. To know their daughter had been the one to find it.

The necklace was still in pieces, but back in their lab in Cairo, someone would piece it back together. The chunky golden scarab would fit perfectly in the palm of her hand. She carefully lifted the small, dog-like amulet. It was slightly smaller than the scarab, and the canine had a slender body like a greyhound, and a long, stiff tail that was forked at the end. She was sure this was a set-animal, the symbol of the Egyptian god, Seth. She stroked the hieroglyphs on the animal's body and the symbols that spelled Zerzura.

Unfortunately, none of the hieroglyphs here made sense. She'd spent hours working on them. They were gibberish.

There was a noise behind her. A scrape of a boot in sand.

She turned, wondering who else had stayed behind.

A fist collided with her face in a vicious blow.

Pain exploded through Layne's cheek and she tasted blood. The blow sent her sprawling into the sand, the set-animal carving falling from her fingers.

Layne couldn't seem to focus. She lay there, her cheek to the sand, trying to clear her head. Her face throbbed and she heard voices talking in Arabic.

A black boot appeared in her line of sight.

A hand reached down and picked up the set-animal.

She swallowed, trying to get her brain working. Then she heard another voice. Deep, cool tones with a clipped British accent that made her blood run cold.

"Move it. I want it done. Fast."

She saw more people come into view. They were all wearing black balaclavas.

They started grabbing the artifacts and stuffing them into canvas bags.

"No." In her head her cry came out loud and outraged. In reality, it was a hoarse whisper.

"Bag everything," the cold voice behind her said.

No. She wasn't letting these thieves steal the artifacts. This was *her* dig and these were her antiquities to safeguard.

She pushed up onto her hands and knees. "Stop." She swung around and kicked at the knee of the man closest to her.

He tipped sideways with a cry.

"Uh-uh." The man with the cold voice stepped into her view. All she saw were his shiny black boots. Before she could do anything else, a hand grabbed her hair and yanked her head back.

The pain made her grit her teeth. Tears stung her eyes. She twisted, trying to pull away from him.

"A spitfire. I do like a feisty woman. Shame I don't have time to play with you."

He was behind her and she couldn't see his face. She tried to jerk away but a hard fist slammed into her head again.

No, no, no. Her vision dimmed, the sound of the thieves' voices receded.

Everything went black.

***

Declan Ward strode into the warehouse, his boots echoing on the scarred concrete. Colorado sunlight streamed through the large windows which offered a fantastic view of downtown Denver.

He was gritty-eyed from lack of sleep, and he was still adjusting to being back on Mountain Time.

He'd gotten in from finishing a job in South East Asia sometime around midnight. He'd unlocked his apartment, stumbled in and stripped, and fallen facedown on his bed.

Now, he was headed to work.

Lucky for him, it paid to be one of the owners. He lived above the warehouse that housed the main offices of Treasure Hunter Security.

Most of the open-plan space that had been a flour mill in a previous life was empty. But at the far end it was a different story.

Flat screens covered the brick wall, all displaying different images and scrolling feeds. Some sleek desks were set up, all covered in high-end computers.

There was a small kitchenette tucked into one corner, and next to that sat some sagging couches that looked like they'd come from a charity shop or some college student's house. Just beyond those, near the large windows, were a pool table and an air hockey table.

"Dec? What are you doing here?"

A small, dark-haired woman popped up from her seat at one of the computers. As always, she was dressed stylishly in dark jeans, a soft red sweater the color of raspberries, and impossibly high heels.

"I work here," he said. "Actually, I own the place. Have the mortgage to prove it."

His sister came right up to him and threw her arms around him. He did the same and absorbed the non-stop energy that Darcy always seemed to emit. She'd never been able to sit still, even as a little girl.

"You just got back. You're supposed to have a week off." She patted his arms and frowned. She had the same gray eyes he did, but hers always seemed to look bluer than his.

"Finished the job, ready for the next one."

Her frown deepened, her hands landing on her hips. "You work too hard."

"Darce, I'm tired, and not really up for this rant this morning." She had this spiel down to a fine art.

She huffed out a breath. "Okay. But I'm not done. Expect an earful later."

Great. He tweaked her nose. He'd done it ever since she was a cute little girl in pigtails and dirt-stained clothes tagging around after him and their brother Callum. Dec knew she hated it.

"Hey, Dec. When did you get back?"

Dec clasped hands with one of his team. Hale

Carter was a big man, topping Dec's six-foot-two by a couple of inches. He'd been a hell of a soldier, was a bit of a genius with anything mechanical, and a guy who managed to smile through it all. He had a wide smile and dark skin courtesy of his African American mother, and a handsome face that drew the ladies like flies.

But Dec knew the man had secrets too, dark ones. Hell, they all did. They'd all been to some terrible places with the SEAL teams. All had seen and done some things that left scars—both physical and mental.

Dec never pried. He offered jobs to the former soldiers who wanted to work—ones where they normally wouldn't get shot at while doing them—and he didn't ask them to reveal all their demons.

Some demons could never be vanquished. He felt his gut tighten. Dec had accepted that long ago.

"Got in last night. Nice to be home." But even as he said the words, Dec knew it wasn't true. He was already feeling the itch to be out, moving, doing something.

It had been two and a half years since he'd left the Navy and stopped heading into the world's worst war zones. Hell, he didn't leave—they'd booted him out. He'd just barely avoided a dishonorable discharge, but they'd wanted him gone anyway, and he didn't blame them.

He shoved his hands into the pockets of his jeans. In those two and a half years, he'd put together Treasure Hunter Security with his brother and sister, and he'd never looked back. Or at least, he tried not to.

Hale was one of their newest recruits and had fit right in.

Dec made his way to the kitchenette and poured a cup of coffee from the pot. Darcy would have made it, which meant it was barely drinkable, but it was black and strong and had caffeine, so it ticked the boxes.

He saw his best friend slouched on one of the couches, his boots on the scarred coffee table and his long legs cased in well-worn jeans. He was flicking a switchblade open and closed.

"Logan."

"Dec."

Logan O'Connor was another SEAL buddy, and the best friend Dec had ever had. They hadn't liked each other at first, but after a particularly brutal mission—followed by an equally brutal bar fight in the seedy backstreets of Bangkok where they had saved each other's backs—they'd formed a bond.

Logan was big as well, the rolled-up sleeves of his shirt showing off his muscled arms and tattoos. From the day they'd left the military, Logan had let his brown hair grow long and shaggy, and his cheeks were covered in scruff. He looked exactly how he was—dangerous and just a little wild.

His friend eyed Dec up and down, then raised a brow. "How was the job?"

"The usual."

Actually, the jobs were never the same, and you were never sure what was going to happen. Providing security to archeological digs, retrieving stolen artifacts, occasionally turning some bad guys over to the authorities, doing museum security, or running remote expeditions for crazy treasure hunters...it kept things interesting.

"Anyone shoot at you?"

The female voice came from over by the computers. Morgan Kincaid sat cross-legged on top of a table. She was one of the few females to pass the rigorous BUD/S training for the Navy SEALs. But when the Navy had refused to let her serve on the teams, she'd left.

The Navy's loss was Dec's gain. Morgan was tough, mean, and hell in a firefight. She was tall, kept her dark hair short, and had a scar down the left side of her face from a knife fight.

"Not this trip," Dec answered.

"Too bad," Morgan murmured.

"All right everyone, listen up." Darcy's voice echoed in the warehouse.

They all headed over to where Darcy stood in front of her screens. Logan and Hale dropped into chairs, Morgan stayed sitting on top of the table, and Dec pressed a hip to a desk and sipped his coffee.

"Where's Cal?" he asked.

"He flew out a few days ago on another job. An anthropologist got snatched by a local tribe in Brazil."

"Hate the jungle," Logan said, his voice a growl.

"And Ronin?" Dec asked.

Ronin Cooper was another full-time Treasure Hunter Security employee. Dec kept a small full-time team and hired on trusted contractors when he needed more muscle.

"Coop's in northern Canada on an expedition."

Dec raised his brows, trying to imagine Ronin in the snow.

Hale hooted with laughter. "Shit, not too many shadows to hide in when you're in the snow."

Dec sipped his coffee again. Ronin Cooper was good at blending into the shadows. You didn't see him coming unless he wanted you to. Another former SEAL, Ronin had gotten out earlier than Dec, and had done some work for the CIA. Lean and intense, Ronin was the scary danger no one saw coming.

Dec settled back against the desk. "What's this new job?"

"An archeological dig in Egypt got attacked yesterday." Darcy pointed a small remote at her screens. A map of Egypt appeared with a red dot out in the Western Desert. "It's being run by the Rhodes University out of Massachusetts."

Dec raised a brow. Rhodes had a hell of an archeological department. They had their fingers in digs all over the world and prided themselves on some of the biggest finds in recent times. Every kid with dreams of being the next Indiana Jones wanted to study at Rhodes.

"The dig is excavating a newly-discovered tomb and surrounding necropolis," Darcy continued. "They'd recently found some artifacts." She pointed again and some images of artifacts appeared. "All gold."

Hale whistled. "Nice."

Dec's muscles tensed. He knew what was coming.

"And now the artifacts are gone." Darcy leaned back on the desk. "The head of the dig was working on the artifacts at the time and was attacked. She survived. And now, we're hired. One, to ensure no more artifacts are stolen, two to ensure the safety of the dig's workers, and three—" Darcy's blue-gray gaze met Dec's "—to recover the stolen artifacts."

Dec felt a muscle tick in his jaw. "It's Anders."

"Ah, hell." Logan tipped his head back. "This is not good."

Hale was frowning. "Who's Anders?"

"Dec has a hard-on for the guy," Morgan muttered.

Dec ignored Logan and Morgan. "Ian Anders. A former British Special Air Service soldier."

Hale's frown deepened. "Heard those SAS guys are hard-core."

"They are," Dec confirmed.

Darcy stepped forward. "Declan and Logan's SEAL team was working a joint mission with Anders' team in the Middle East."

"Caught the sadistic fucker torturing locals." Even now, the screams and moans of those people came back to Dec. A nightmare he couldn't seem to outrun. "He kept them hidden, visited them every few days. Men, women...children." Dec let out a breath. "No idea how long he'd had them there."

"You saved them?" Hale said.

"No." Dec stood and took his mug to the sink. He

tipped the coffee he could no longer stomach down the drain.

"You did the right thing, Dec," Logan growled.

Silence fell. Dec was not going to talk about this.

Darcy cleared her throat. "The British Military gave Anders a slap on the wrist."

"Shit," Hale said. "So what's he got to do with stolen artifacts?"

"When he left the SAS, he got into black-market antiquities," Declan said. "We've run into him a few times on jobs."

"The guy is whacked," Logan added. "He likes to hurt and kill. And he likes the pretty cash he gets for selling artifacts."

"And you think this is his work?" Hale looked at the screens.

Dec had learned to trust his gut. Sometimes despite the facts or evidence, despite the fact you had nothing else to go on. "Yeah, it's Anders."

"Logan, Morgan, and Hale, this is your assignment," Darcy said. "You'll head to Egypt to meet Dr. Layne Rush."

Another screen filled with a photo of a woman.

Dec blinked, feeling his belly clench, even though he'd never seen this woman before.

He wasn't even sure what warranted the gut-deep response. She was attractive, but not the most beautiful woman he'd ever seen. In the photo, she had sunglasses pushed up on her dark hair. Her hair was chocolate brown and straight as a ruler. It brushed her shoulders, except for the bangs cut bluntly just across her eyes. Her skin was so incredibly clear, not a blemish on it, and her eyes were hazel.

She had smart stamped all over her. *Hell*. Dec had a thing for smart women.

But he usually steered well clear. He wasn't made for hearts and rainbows. He'd just seen too much and done too much. His relationships generally lasted one night, and he enjoyed women who wanted the same as him—uncomplicated, no-strings sex.

"I'm going." Dec's voice echoed in the warehouse.

Darcy's beautiful face got a pinched look. "Declan—"

"No arguments, Darce. I'm going."

"You're going because of Anders," she said.

Dec glanced at the photo of Dr. Rush. "I'm going to pack."

His sister sighed and looked at Dec. "You're sure you won't change your mind."

"Nope."

Another sigh. "The jet's fueled and waiting. Logan, please keep him out of trouble."

Logan snorted. "I'm good, but I'm not that good."

Darcy shook her head. "All of you, have a good trip…and stay safe. Please."

Dec smiled, trying to break the tension. "You know me."

A resigned look crossed her face. "Yes. Unfortunately, I do. So when the trouble hits, call me."

Chapter Two

Layne walked down a crowded street in the Khan el-Khalili, absorbing the sights, smells and sounds of Cairo's market district. Someone nearby was cooking falafel, which made her stomach grumble and reminded her she'd only had coffee for breakfast.

The narrow street was lined with shops whose wares spilled out into the street. Walls of colored fabric, shelves filled with souvenirs and ornaments, another with beautiful colored lanterns. All around were the sounds of hawkers calling out their wares and the rush of people—some locals and others obviously tourists. One local man walked past, balancing a huge tray of Egyptian flatbread on his head.

She loved Cairo's bazaar district with its hustle and bustle. Beneath the tourist trappings was a deep sense of history. It had been built on the site of a mausoleum, and the sultans had made it a place of commerce and trade. Even today, it was still an important place for the locals. There were numerous traditional workshops in the Khan el-Khalili, like the goldsmiths and the silver merchants.

And there were also several of her local contacts who traded in antiquities.

She'd already visited them. Her jaw clenched. No one had seen her stolen artifacts. They'd all promised her that if any of them came up on the market, they'd contact her.

But Layne wasn't planning on holding her breath.

She scowled, anger flooding her like a shot of lava to the veins. She couldn't believe someone had been brazen enough to just waltz into her dig and steal valuable pieces of history like they were the tourist trinkets surrounding her.

Layne reached up and touched her cheek. It was now a spectacular black and green from the bruising. And a constant reminder of her failure.

Her bosses back at the university had been incensed and horrified to find out about the theft. They'd been sympathetic, but she could read between the lines of the carefully crafted responses.

This was a black mark on her record.

She breathed in a long breath. She wanted her dig to be a success, but more than that, she wanted to ensure everything they found could be studied and find a home in museums where anyone could go and see it.

She remembered her mother holding her hand, wandering their local museum. It had been one of the things that had ignited Layne's love of history. She'd been too young then to understand the museum was free, and the only place her mother could afford to take her.

Anyway, now the university was on edge, and in response to the theft and attack on her, they'd hired a specialized security firm.

Layne's scowl deepened, making her bruise throb. It was all she needed. Untrained people trampling her dig, issuing orders in the name of security, and getting in her way.

Still, if it helped safeguard the artifacts and keep her team safe, she wasn't going to argue.

She kept walking. The university's Cairo office and lab were a few blocks away. She'd spend the rest of the day there, another night in the city waiting for the security team to arrive, then head back to the dig.

Already she was itching to be back there.

She paused as a group of men in local jellabiya robes cut across in front of her.

It was then she felt a strange prickling at the back of her neck.

Someone was watching her.

She stood frozen for a second. This had to just be a bad reaction to being attacked.

Still, she slowly turned her head. Like she was looking at the nearby store and its wall of colored scarves and jewelry.

Then she spotted him.

She looked away, but the short glimpse was enough for her to catalogue the dark, intense man. Tan cargo pants, and a navy-blue T-shirt that stretched over a lean, muscled chest and toned biceps. Dark glasses and dark hair cut short.

He was definitely watching her.

Layne picked up speed. She knew these streets better than she knew her own neighborhood around the university. Hell, she spent more time here than her barely used apartment.

Her heart was beating hard, reminding her starkly of lying facedown in the sand while those men took her artifacts.

But she shoved the memory aside. If this man knew where her artifacts were, she was going to find out.

She ducked down an alley. It was lined with tiny, overcrowded stalls. She glanced over her shoulder and saw the man was following. She smiled.

Layne followed a twisting path through the market. Then she quickly doubled back.

She ducked through a shortcut covered by a stall selling bad reproductions of Tutankhamun's mask and Nefertiti's bust. She ducked out into the neighboring alley and came back around.

She spied the man ahead of her now, hands on his lean hips, looking around. His lips were moving and she got the distinct impression he was cursing.

She reached into the small courier bag she had draped over her body. She pulled out her tube of lip gloss and held it in her hand. She came up behind him and jabbed it in his lower back.

"Don't move," she said quietly. "I don't want to hurt you, but I do want to know why you're following me."

When he shifted his weight, like he was going to spin around, she jabbed him harder.

"I've already had someone punch me in the face and knock me out this week, so I'm not in a particularly good mood. You don't want to test me."

***

She'd gotten the drop on him. *Damn.*

Dec couldn't believe it. Taken in by an archeologist. If Logan ever found out, Dec would never live it down.

He weighed his options. Despite whatever weapon she was carrying—and despite the firm determination in her voice—he was fairly certain Dr. Rush wasn't going to shoot him in the middle of a crowded Cairo market.

Dec spun. He grabbed her wrist and heard her gasp. As he snatched the weapon, he got a glimpse of wide, green-gold eyes under blunt bangs. Then the little spitfire moved, bringing her knee up and aiming for his crotch.

He wrapped his arms around her, spun, and pushed her through a wall of fabric. Somewhere nearby, a shopkeeper squawked. Dec kept going until he had her pressed up against a stone wall, his body pinning hers there so she couldn't use her knee.

She still fought, though, wriggling and twisting.

"Stop, before you hurt yourself," he growled.

She kept fighting.

"Dr. Rush, I'm not going to hurt you."

She stilled, her mutinous gaze meeting his. "Let me go."

He ignored her and lifted the tiny thing in his hand. His eyebrows shot upward, embarrassment flooding him. "Lipstick? You pretended you were going to shoot me with lipstick?"

She sniffed. "It's lip gloss. And I never said I was going to shoot you. I said I didn't want to *hurt* you." She frowned. "I'm rapidly thinking about changing my mind, though."

Dec shook his head with reluctant admiration. "Dr. Rush, you can try, but I don't recommend it."

Her frown deepened, and he realized she had really full lips that were at odds with the rest of her face, with its sharp cheekbones and pointed chin. Pressed up against her, he felt tightly-packed curves and full breasts. His cock stirred and he cursed mentally.

"Who are you?" she demanded.

"Declan Ward. Treasure Hunter Security."

Her eyes widened. "The new security specialist." She pushed at his chest.

Dec stepped back, and for a second, missed the warmth of her.

"Why the hell were you stalking me?" she snapped.

"I was checking you out. It's part of my job."

Now her eyebrows rose, disappearing under her bangs. "You think *I* have something to do with the theft of my artifacts?"

Yep, she was smart. He saw the intelligence glittering in those fascinating hazel eyes of hers. Large flecks of gold glimmered against the deep green.

Her voice rose. "You think I did this to myself?" She waved at her cheek.

The ugly bruise made his gut harden. In the photo, he'd noted her clear, almost-translucent skin. Up close, on her right cheek, that skin was even more attractive. He could even make out the delicate blue veins beneath her skin. The skin of her left cheek, however, was marred by a bruise that was an ugly reminder that someone had hurt her.

That Ian Anders had hurt her.

"Look Mr. Ward, I don't know who the hell you think you are." She poked him in the center of his chest. "But I have dedicated my life to my career. To finding, safeguarding, and studying history and its artifacts. I am in charge of this dig, and I have a hell of a lot riding on it. I wouldn't jeopardize the biggest opportunity of my career, not to mention my personal integrity, to sell off antiquities."

There was passion in Dr. Rush. He saw it burning in her eyes, heard it overflowing in her voice as she talked about her work.

God, when had he felt anything like that? Most days, he felt nothing.

Focus, Ward. "I'm doing my job, Dr. Rush. You want your artifacts back? You want to make sure no more go missing?"

Her tight shoulders sagged. "Yes."

"Then I'm going to leave no stone unturned. I investigate everyone, until I know every little thing about them. Where they live, how much money they have in the bank, who their friends are, hell, even what color their panties are."

Her lips pressed into a straight line. "Okay, I guess we're on the same page, then."

"And the same team."

"I'll save you some work." She tucked her hair back behind her ears. "I live in Rhodes, Massachusetts, I have fifty-seven thousand dollars in savings in the bank but more than that in stocks and retirement savings. I don't have a lot of time for socializing, so my friends are the people I work with. My underwear is not up for discussion."

"You mean you keep an apartment near the university that you barely use, you have sixty-two thousand in stocks and 401K, and you're closest to your assistant Piper Ross." He couldn't resist a small smile. "And you prefer black lace underwear."

Her mouth dropped open and she stared at him. "I don't know whether to be impressed or to hit you."

"How about we go somewhere where we can talk?" He glanced around. There were too many people here, and while no one appeared to be paying them any attention, he didn't want someone to overhear what he had to say.

She nodded. "There's a small café around the corner where I go a lot."

Moments later, they'd found seats in a crowded café. Wooden chairs and tables were packed close together in the small space. The butter-colored walls were filled with carved wooden decorations and mirrors. Most of the clientele were locals, wearing regular clothes, but a few were dressed in simple, light-colored robes, and many sat, sucking on the end of the shisha pipes popular in Egypt. The tall, elegant glass waterpipes for smoking flavored tobacco sat on the floor beside each table.

Dec sat on the small chair and edged forward, his knees bumping slim legs under the table. A harried waiter dropped off a coffee for Dec, and a mint tea for Dr. Rush. The tea was in a tall glass, rimmed with gold. Dec's coffee was of the local variety—he'd picked up a taste for the strong coffee after spending a lot of time in the Middle East. He lifted the small brass pot and poured the coffee into his cup, the bold scent hitting him.

Dr. Rush sipped her tea. "So, you're planning to investigate all of my team?"

"I already am. I have my team Stateside running checks. If anyone's opened an offshore account or received a large sum of money recently, my tech expert will find it."

The lovely doctor's eyebrows rose. "He must be good."

"She is."

Rush's fingers tightened on her cup. "What if this was just random—?"

"It wasn't. You must know that a lot of digs in the area have been hit over the last few months. Especially high-profile ones."

She nodded. "They did seem to know what they were doing." She shivered.

He saw the shadows, recognized them. He wanted to reach out and place his hand on hers.

Stupid. Dec was good at protecting, crap at providing comfort. "No one is going to hurt you again."

She swallowed. "No. Because this time, I'll be better prepared."

He nodded. "And I'm going to help you with that. Once we get to the dig site, my team and I will do a security assessment and implement any recommendations—"

"Whoa, hang on, Mr. Security Expert. It is still *my* dig and I have work to do. Any recommendations, you run them past me first."

Dec stirred his coffee. "Security matters fall under my control, Dr. Rush. Your bosses have already given the okay for me to do whatever I need to do to safeguard you, your team, and the artifacts."

She huffed out a breath. "I'm not going to stop you from doing that, hell, I *want* you to do that. But can you guarantee your security team won't hamper our work, or possibly endanger the integrity of our studies—?"

"Nope. Lives come first. Then the valuables. If I have to trample on your dig while I do that, sorry."

She stared at him. "You like giving orders, don't you, Mr. Ward?"

"It's Declan. We're going to be spending a whole lot of time together, so use it. Mr. Ward makes me think of my dad." He sipped his coffee, liking the blush of heated color in her cheeks. "And yes, I've been giving orders ever since they gave me my own SEAL team."

Rush looked upward. "A SEAL. I should have known. I knew you were Special Forces, but of course, you have to be one of the biggest and baddest of them all."

He studied her. He was used to lots of reactions from women in regards to his former career. Some were intrigued in an "I'm going to drag you to bed" kind of way. Others were often intimidated.

But the lovely Dr. Rush was neither. She just absorbed the information as a fact and didn't look particularly impressed.

"And don't worry about your dig, Rush. We specialize in this kind of work...we know not to trample the archeology."

"Okay, Mr. Ward...Declan. Once we get to the dig, I'll listen to the security recommendations you have."

She'd do more than listen. Still, he'd prefer they worked together, not against each other.

He leaned forward. "I also wanted to ask you about the attack. Any details you remember that might help me?"

She went tense and set her glass down.

He saw it—the horror, the helplessness—all over her face. He hated to make her relive it. "I'm sorry—"

"No." She shook her head, visibly pulling herself together. "I'll tell you what I can."

Dec was impressed. She locked down her fear and memories, and was looking at him, face composed. A glint of steel in her eye. "Good, okay. How many thieves?"

A crease appeared between her brows. "Four, maybe five. I didn't see them all. Especially after I got hit."

Dec pulled out a small notepad and jotted some notes. "Locals?"

"I think so. They spoke Arabic. Except for the man in charge." She shivered, her hands clenching together. "My cheek was hurting and I was having trouble focusing. But his voice... I'd remember it anywhere."

This time Dec couldn't stop himself. He put his hand on hers and squeezed. "You're doing well. What about this guy?"

"He had a British accent. And his voice was cold, empty." She gave a small laugh. "God, it sounds so cliché. The cold British bad guy." She looked up and when she saw Dec's face, her smile vanished. "You know who he is."

Dammit. Dec must really be losing his edge. His guys joked no one could read his poker face, unless he wanted them to. "His name is Anders. Ian Anders."

"He's a thief?"

"He's a former soldier, British Special Forces. He moved into stealing antiquities to sell on the black market a few years ago. He usually does the job himself, and is damn good at sneaking in and out." Dec wasn't sure how much to tell her. He didn't want to frighten her more than she already was. But staring into her face, he knew Dr. Layne Rush was made of pretty tough stuff. And the more information she had, the better off she'd be. "He usually leaves a few dead bodies behind, as well. In fact, he enjoys it."

She gasped, her hands tightening, her knuckles white. "He said he wished he had more time to play before he knocked me out."

Dec wasn't sure what that meant, but he didn't like it. He hadn't heard of Anders working with a team before. Or leaving people alive. All of this sounded off. "He possibly just wanted to keep you quiet."

"I…" Her voice cracked. "In that moment, I had no idea what would happen. If they'd take me, kill me…"

"Hey." Dec tipped her chin up and wasn't surprised to find the skin under her jaw was soft as hell. He had no idea how a woman who spent months on remote digs in harsh conditions had this baby-fine skin. "You're okay. Nothing's going to happen to you."

She pulled in a breath. "So, this Anders guy stole my artifacts."

"Yes. But he doesn't usually work with a team—"

"Or leave people alive," she added.

"Yeah." It was a bit of a mystery, and Dec hated mysteries. "I'm working to track him and your artifacts down." Dec's phone rang. "Sorry." He glanced at the screen. "It's my man, Logan, he's working this job with me. Logan, what have you got?"

"Dec. Just got a call from Hasan Kelada. Said he has a pretty little piece of gold you might want to take a look at."

Yes. "Thanks, Logan. I'll check it out."

Dec flicked his phone off and looked at Rush. "An antiquities dealer I know here in Cairo thinks he just purchased one of your artifacts."

Dr. Rush's eyes widened. "I just spent the morning questioning dealers I know. They said they hadn't seen or heard anything."

Dec pressed his tongue to his teeth. "I'm guessing your dealers are all legitimate."

She nodded. "Of course."

"My guy is…not."

Her gaze narrowed. "Black market?"

"More gray with a few shades of brown. Come on." Dec stood. "Let's go pay him a visit."

Chapter Three

Layne stepped into the overcrowded shop, trying to fight back her righteous anger.

She was going to visit a black-market dealer. Her stomach was turning circles. Someone who took important, valuable pieces of history and sold them for their own personal gain.

The shop looked like any other one in the Khan el-Khalili. It was crammed full of cheap replicas of Tut's mask, statues, Bastet cats, and seated scribes. Gaudy papyri covered the walls. One side of the store was filled with shisha pipes. She wondered how the hell the tourists got those home on the plane.

An older Egyptian lady watched them from the back of the shop.

Declan stepped forward and to Layne's shock, spoke in perfect Arabic. He traded greetings with the woman, even got a smile out of her, then she waved them through a door in the back.

They walked down a dingy hall.

"You speak Arabic?" she asked, studying him.

"Picked it up on the teams."

Her gaze narrowed. His face would probably be considered handsome by some. But no one would accuse him of being pretty. His features had a hard, sharp edge that matched the intensity of his gunmetal-gray eyes. His nose was slightly crooked and she wondered how he'd broken it.

Well, the man was sure blowing her idea of muscled, macho SEALs who were all brawn and no brains out of the water.

At the end of the hall, a burly man leaned against the wall, watching them get closer. He looked bored, but Layne saw the pistol holstered at his hip, and she tensed.

The man didn't say anything to them, just opened the door.

Inside was like stepping into a different world. Layne gasped, pressing a hand to her chest.

It was a small gallery—sleek and polished, where the shop at the front was crowded and worn. The floor was glossy tiles, the walls painted a pearl-gray, and rows of glass display cabinets filled the space. Each was illuminated with discreet lights. Some of the cases were empty and some were not.

Layne hurried over to the first case, her mouth going dry. "Declan, look at this! It's an Eye of Horus." It was an ornate eye with graceful swirls made of gold and inlaid with precious stones. Also called a wadjet, it was a symbol of protection, and this one was in pristine condition. "This is museum-worthy."

"Rush, we're here to get Hasan's help. If you berate him about this, he might just show us the door."

"But—"

"You want your artifacts back? You want to stop Anders?"

She huffed out a breath. "I'm guessing you're going to be annoying. A huge pain in my...side."

A faint smile on his lips. "Count on it."

She wandered down the row of display cases. A bronze of the goddess Hathor. Canopic jars. Sets of amulets. Pottery. Gold jewelry. She flexed her hands. These were some of the best quality pieces she'd seen. "These should all be in museums."

"Where they'll be crowded in with other artifacts, or stored in boxes in dusty back rooms?"

The new, accented voice made her spin.

The man was an older, portly Egyptian with a head full of thick gray hair and a strong-boned face.

"No, studied and admired by thousands." Beside her, she heard Declan sigh. "And by more than just one person with deep pockets."

The man moved forward, a faint smile on his face. "Have you visited some of my country's museums? Dark, dusty, overcrowded, limited security."

She pursed her lips. He wasn't wrong. But that didn't make it right for people to sell them on the black market.

"The Egyptian Museum in Cairo alone has over one hundred and twenty thousand artifacts. I can tell you only a small fraction are on display." He waved a hand. "The rest molder away."

"Hasan, good to see you." Declan came forward to shake hands with the man.

"You too, Declan," the man said warmly. "It's been too long, my friend."

"Hasan, this is Dr. Layne Rush. Rush, Hasan Kelada."

Hasan's bushy eyebrows rose. "Rush? You're from Rhodes University."

She gave him a stiff nod.

"And you run the new dig out near Dakhla." Now the man's eyes widened. "My new acquisition..."

"Was likely stolen from my dig," Layne said.

Declan pressed a hand to her shoulder. "Hasan, can we see it?"

"Of course, of course." He waved them toward a door. "Come into my office."

Hasan's office was nothing like the gallery. A battered wooden desk dominated the space and it was covered in piles of papers and books.

The dealer moved to the back wall and lifted a lovely, framed papyrus showing the famous weighing of the heart scene from the Book of the Dead off the wall. Behind it was a state-of-the-art safe. She watched him enter a code and press his palm to a pad. Biometrics. It was really impressive. She scowled to herself. Who knew that black-market dealers took security of stolen goods so seriously?

Hasan pulled out a tray and set it on his desk.

Layne gasped. "My set-animal amulet!"

"*Egypt's* set-animal amulet, Dr. Rush," Hasan said dryly.

"Of course. But it was *my* job to safeguard it

until the Ministry of Antiquities—"

"Stuffs it in dusty storage. Somewhere to never see the light of day again."

Her hands balled. "It isn't for you to decide."

"I believe in safeguarding my country's artifacts too, Dr. Rush. But I do it my way, not the bureaucrats' way. I am doing what I think is best."

She raised a brow. "And turning a profit while you do it."

He shot her a charming smile. "A man needs to feed his family."

"Mr. Kalada, I'm pretty sure that Rolex on your wrist isn't a cheap knockoff."

He just smiled at her again.

Declan stepped forward. "Okay, how about you two agree to disagree? Layne, you're sure this is from your dig?"

She touched the edge of the animal, reading the glyphs inscribed on it. "Absolutely."

Declan pinned his gaze on Hasan. "Who sold it to you?"

"A man I hadn't done business with before. A British man. Not the friendliest fellow."

Layne saw Declan tense.

"He only offered you this?" Declan gestured at the amulet.

"Yes. Said it was the last item in the lot he was selling." Hasan sank into his desk chair. "But he said he has more pieces coming. Things of far better quality than this." Hasan laughed, a big bold sound. "He said he was on the verge of discovering Zerzura." The dealer shook his head. "Many crazy foreigners come to Egypt to try and find the lost oasis."

"It's just a myth," Layne said.

Hasan nodded. "That is one thing we can agree on, Dr. Rush."

"Zerzura?" Declan said with a frown.

"You don't know the legend of Zerzura?" Hasan said. "The White City in the desert? A group of British adventurers back during World War II formed the Zerzura Club, and tried to find this treasure-filled city." Hasan's brow creased. "And there was a Hungarian as well, they made a movie about his life."

Layne nodded. "The adventurers found lots of caves filled with prehistoric cave paintings, around the border with Egypt and Libya. But they never found Zerzura. The legend begins farther back than that, though. Ancient writings tell of a caravan that sets out from the Nile, heading to the oases. A sandstorm hits. One traveler barely survives, and once the storm has passed, everything looks different. He's rescued by the Zerzurans—fair-skinned, blue-eyed people who live in a fantastic white city."

"Fair-skinned?" Declan raised a brow. "Unlikely out here."

"Did you know that Ramses II and several other pharaohs were fair-skinned with red hair?" Layne said.

"Really?" Declan glanced at Hasan.

The Egyptian man nodded. "DNA analysis links Tutankhamun to Western European ancestors. My country was a melting pot of peoples."

Layne hurried on. She might doubt Zerzura existed, but she loved the tale her parents had told her so many times. "Ancient Egyptians called themselves red men, but there were clearly paler-skinned people in the mix."

"Okay," Declan said, shoving his hands in his pockets. "Why? Why build a city way out in the middle of a dangerous desert, far from the Nile and what passed for civilization back then?"

Layne opened her mouth, closed it. "I don't know."

"I doubt it was real," Hasan said. "A myth. Like so many things mentioned in Ancient Egyptian mythology."

"My research leads me to suspect it has something to do with the god Seth," Layne added.

"Really?" Hasan leaned forward.

"His symbol is right there." She waved at the set-animal. "And he was god of the Western Desert. I believe Zerzura was his mythological home."

Hasan nodded. "A good theory."

"Seth?" Declan said. "The god of destruction?"

Layne huffed out a breath. "Seth is seriously misunderstood. In early texts, he was considered a warrior and a protector."

"He did slay the demon snake, Apep," Hasan said, nodding.

"He was vilified in later years," Layne said. "When Upper and Lower Egypt joined, Seth was the god of Upper Egypt. But people in Lower Egypt, the winners in the conflict, worshipped Osiris and his son Horus. They clearly felt the need to demonize Seth and install their own gods as the righteous victors."

"Horus. The falcon god," Declan said.

"You have a pretty decent knowledge of Egyptian history," she said.

He shrugged. "I work around a lot of historical artifacts. It rubs off. Besides, my parents...work in the history field, too."

Layne tucked her hair behind her ear, enjoying sharing her thoughts. "The legends surrounding Seth changed. They say he was jealous and killed his brother, Osiris, and chopped his body into pieces and spread them across Egypt. It's the most famous myth in Egyptian history. Osiris' wife, Isis, found the pieces and used her magic to bring him back to life long enough to conceive a child. Horus. Seth then battled his nephew for the throne."

"So the Horus followers started bad-mouthing Seth?" Declan gave a thoughtful nod. "Propaganda."

"Exactly. Seth got relegated to being god of the desert, destruction, storms, foreigners, etc. Anything scary."

"So, there is a myth about a lost oasis filled with treasure, and you think it was the home of Seth, a demonized god." Declan shook his head. "The world is littered with myths and legends of lost cities, sunken cities, destroyed cities...all of them filled with treasure."

Layne nodded. "And lost cities are for fools."

"I thought you'd made a few legendary discoveries, Rush?"

Just how much did he know about her? "All on well-researched, legitimate digs. I don't go dashing into jungles and deserts on a whim and a myth."

"Nor does Anders. Unfortunately, he's no fool." Declan scowled at the wall, lost in thought.

Layne sensed something. Declan and this Anders had some sort of history, and from the bad vibes coming off Declan, it couldn't have been good.

"Anders is either really desperate, or he has something that makes him think Zerzura is real," Declan said.

Layne's heartbeat tripped. How amazing would it be if Zerzura was real? Her mother's voice echoed in her head. *You have to believe in wonderful things, Laynie. Or life isn't worth living.*

Well, Layne had stopped believing the day she'd stepped in her parents' blood.

Declan looked at his friend. "Hasan, this man, Anders, is dangerous. Steer clear if you can, tread carefully if you can't."

The dealer nodded. "I appreciate the warning, although I have dealt with some unsavory characters before."

"I bet," Layne said dryly. "But you still do business with them."

"Dr. Rush, the way I see it, I re-acquire artifacts from them, and in my own way, stop those artifacts from disappearing for good or being damaged. I try to sell them on to reputable collectors and sometimes, even a few museums. I'm doing the same job as you, safeguarding our history."

Layne didn't say anything.

Hasan grinned. "I am really just carrying on the family business—"

Declan groaned. "No, Hasan. Just keep that story to yourself."

The man ignored Declan. "—like my grave-robber ancestors before me."

Layne's mouth dropped open. "Grave robbers?"

"Yes. But don't worry, I don't raid tombs." He winked.

Layne couldn't help but laugh, but she smothered it quickly. "You aren't going to convince me that what you do is right, Hasan."

He sighed. "I see that. Declan, sadly, your lady is not very impressed with me."

"I think she's pretty hard to impress, Hasan." Declan clapped the man on the shoulder. "If Anders contacts you again, you call me, okay?"

"I will."

"And be careful."

"I will, old friend. You, too."

Declan pressed a hip to the desk. "Now...how much for the artifact?"

Hasan's lips morphed into a knowing grin.

Layne spluttered. "You aren't paying him—"

"I paid a lot of money for it." Hasan straightened. "And I have a family to feed."

Declan shook his head. "Let's negotiate."

Layne closed her eyes and wondered how she'd even ended up here.

***

Darcy Ward took a sip of her chai tea latte, then reached across the desk and tapped on the keyboard. A screen on the wall flashed and the new search initiated.

She leaned back in her chair, crossed her legs and swung her foot. Nothing had popped up yet on the background searches for the archeologists. They all looked clean, well, so far. She set her favorite red mug down, her mind ticking over the things she still needed to do. She still had to look into the local workers, which was a bit trickier since they were foreign nationals. She waggled her fingers. Luckily she liked tricky.

Glancing at the farthest screen to the left, she checked on all the THS members in the field. Everyone had checked in. And everyone was out on jobs which meant the office was blissfully peaceful.

She loved having the place to herself. Just her and her computers. She'd outgrown the geeky, unbearably shy teenager she'd been, but something about being hunched over her computer, hard drive whirring, and just her wits against a problem sang to her.

While the searches were running, she needed to take care of some of the business things—accounts, expenses, payroll. She frowned. Callum had charged a speedboat rental to the company account. She rolled her eyes. She was damn sure it would have been completely unnecessary, but her brother liked to go fast. Too fast.

But right now, she was more worried about Declan. He and Anders...it was just a bad combination. She tapped the keyboard, pulling up some files. She prayed Declan didn't take any unnecessary risks. He wasn't the same easy-going man who'd joined the Navy so many years ago. She knew everything he'd been through had changed him, but she sometimes wished he'd smile more.

The front door clicked open and footsteps sounded, echoing in the warehouse. Prospective customers? She stood and turned with a smile. It withered away in a second.

Two men were crossing the space toward her. One, she hadn't seen before. The other was staring right at her, his green eyes intense.

A dark suit draped his well-built physique. His thick, brown hair was cut short and he had a shadow of scruff across his hard jaw. Here was another man who never smiled. She couldn't see the bulge of his handgun, but she knew he had a holster under his jacket.

Why did the most annoying man in the world have to look so damn good?

"Ms. Ward."

Ugh, the way he said her name set her on edge. "Special Agent Burke."

She watched as his gaze lifted from her and scanned the warehouse.

Special Agent Alastair Burke was part of the FBI's specialized Art Crime Team. The group— made up of a small team of agents—was in charge of investigating art theft and recovering stolen artifacts. He'd been equal parts roadblock and ally to Treasure Hunter Security over the years. Burke had stonewalled THS before on certain jobs. She forced her face to stay cool and composed. He might feed Dec and Cal information sometimes, but for her, it didn't outweigh the times he was a damn thorn in their side.

Besides, the way he looked at the office, looked at her... The man just thought he was superior to everyone else.

"I need to speak to Declan."

Darcy crossed her arms over her chest. "Sorry. He's not here."

Burke's face was impassive. "He's in Egypt. On the Rhodes dig."

She hated that he always had information he shouldn't. She guessed that's what made him good at his job, but it still irritated. She stayed silent and kept her gaze on his.

Burke sighed. "I need his number."

"You're the fancy special agent, can't you find out his number?"

Burke's eyes narrowed and he stepped closer to her. So close she felt the heat radiating off him and his crisp, clean cologne hit her senses.

"You want me to arrest you for obstructing—"

The other man moved now. He smiled at her and Darcy noted he was younger than Burke with a clean-cut face and what could be some Indian heritage. "We're sorry to intrude, Ms. Ward. I'm Special Agent Thomas Singh. We have information we think your brother might need."

"Are you the good agent to his bad agent?" She nodded at Burke.

Agent Singh's smile widened. "He can't do good agent. Just not capable. So I'm usually stuck with it, although I do a mean bad agent." His smile morphed into a scowl.

"Singh," Burke growled. Then his laser-sharp gaze pinned her again. "It's about Ian Anders."

Darcy froze.

"And Silk Road."

She hissed out a breath. She didn't know much about the shadowy black-market antiquities ring. Not for lack of trying. But even with her best hacking, she'd discovered very little about them. She knew she didn't want them messing with her brother.

"I can talk to Dec. Ask him if I can give you his number."

Burke stepped closer and it made Darcy hate the fact she was short, even in her heels.

"I could force you to give it to me."

She lifted her chin. "Try it."

He stared down at her.

"Uh...no, that's fine," Agent Singh said. "We'll wait while you call your brother."

Darcy yanked her Bluetooth headset on and walked across the warehouse, taking a few deep breaths.

But she still felt Burke's gaze on her.

***

Declan stepped out onto the street and slipped his sunglasses on.

"I cannot believe how much you paid for it."

He could practically feel the anger wafting off Rush. He eyed her and her flushed cheeks. She was kind of cute when she was riled up.

"I know you don't like it, but we got your artifact back." It was safely wrapped and tucked into his backpack. "And Hasan will let us know if Anders comes back."

She gave a resigned nod and together they headed down the street. "So, you and this Anders have a history."

Dec stiffened and didn't look at her. She hadn't made it a question. "Yes."

"That's it? That's all you're going to tell me?"

He stopped and swung her around to face him. "Anders is dangerous and you're damned lucky to be alive. That's all you need to know."

She stared at Dec for a second. "You can just say 'I don't want to talk about it.'" She pulled her arm from his grip. "So, what now?"

Dec exhaled a long breath, trying to push back the dark anger churning in him. "I've already sent a text to my tech expert to find out anything new on Anders. I need to know why he's after Zerzura, and why he's going off his usual script." It made Declan nervous. Anders was dangerous enough without adding unpredictable and desperate to the mix.

"Well, the university offices are a few blocks from here," Layne said.

They were halfway there when Dec felt a tingle along his senses. He slowed and scanned the street, but nothing stood out in the hustle and bustle.

His phone rang, vibrating in his pocket. "Hang on, Rush." He opened his phone. "Ward."

"Dec, it's Darcy. How's Egypt?"

"Warm."

His sister sighed. "Always a man of many words."

"Shut it. What have you got for me?"

"He who thinks he is far better than all of us paid me a visit." Darcy's voice was sharp and annoyed. "He wants to talk to you."

"I take it you're talking about Special Agent Burke."

"God, that man is so fricking annoying. He talks to me like I'm an idiot."

"He talks like an FBI agent." If Burke wanted to talk, then he had information. "Okay, Darce, give him my number."

"Roger that. You please deal with him, so I don't have to." His sister hung up.

"Problem?" Layne asked.

"Nope. It might be a break." Like clockwork, his phone rang. "Ward."

"Ward, it's Burke. Heard you're after Anders." Burke's voice was grim.

"Yeah. He attacked a dig in Egypt. We've been hired to get the stolen items back and provide security for the dig."

"You and Anders don't mix, Ward."

"Appreciate the concern. Makes me feel all warm and fuzzy."

"Fuck you," Burke said good-naturedly. "Word is, Anders is in deep."

"To who?"

"To whom," he heard Layne mutter under her breath.

"No one warm and fuzzy," Burke replied. "You know I've been investigating this global black-market ring, they call themselves the Silk Road. I've never gotten close to the head of it. Don't know who the main players are." A frustrated sound. "But Anders has been selling to them and it sounds like he borrowed money from them at some stage. Money he's having trouble repaying."

"Shit."

"Yeah. If he doesn't pay them back to the tune of twenty million in the next month, he'll be dead. These people don't dick around. The last one of their guys who screwed them over was found with his head stuck on a spike outside the Tower of London."

Dec winced. "Anders appears to be going after the lost city of Zerzura."

"Shit. He must be feeling the heat." Burke paused. "Zerzura isn't real, right?"

"So the experts tell me." He saw Layne watching him steadily. No doubt piecing everything together from her side of the conversation.

"He might make mistakes, then, Ward," Burke said. "You might be able to finally nab him."

Dec grunted. "Or it just makes him even more dangerous."

"Tread lightly. You need help, give me a call. I have some friends in Interpol who could help you out. They'd be very happy to get their hands on Anders."

"Got it. Burke...thanks for the info."

"You know I'm keeping a tab. You'll owe me."

"Screw you." Dec ended the call. But he knew he had a small debt owing to the FBI agent, and if and when Burke came calling, Dec wouldn't hesitate to help the man. Even if he did drive Darcy crazy.

"What?" Layne demanded.

"That was my contact at the FBI. Said Anders is in deep debt to some very nasty people. He's desperate."

"That's not good."

"No. Rush, I think it's time we head to your dig."

"The train to Luxor leaves this afternoon. We have to overnight on the train, and then it's several hours' drive in a four wheel drive to get to the dig site."

He smiled. "I have my company jet on standby at Cairo airport."

Now her mouth dropped open again. God, Dec was getting a real kick out of surprising Dr. Rush. "The university is paying me very well to keep you and its artifacts safe."

But as they headed off down the street, Dec once again got the feeling they were being watched.

Anders wasn't gone. He was just biding his time.

Chapter Four

Layne stepped out onto the tarmac at Cairo Airport and spotted the sleek black jet.

Wow. She traveled a lot—but it was always in narrow Economy seats, or crammed into the back of small charter planes.

"Come on, Rush." Declan walked two steps ahead of her. "I'll introduce you to the team."

She followed him up the steps and ducked inside.

She'd expected leather seats and plush décor, but this jet had been outfitted very differently. The seats were, indeed, leather, but other than that, there were sleek computer screens along one wall and lots of built-in storage compartments beneath.

But what dominated the small aircraft were the three tall people lounging around.

They all called out hellos to Declan, but Layne felt her eyes widen. She'd never seen a more dangerous-looking, intimidating crew in her life.

"Everyone, this is Dr. Layne Rush," Declan said. "She's head of the dig, from Rhodes University."

She felt all eyes on her, assessing. She got the feeling these people spent all their time assessing, calculating, and planning to attack. "Hi."

"Rush, this guy here is Logan O'Connor."

The big man, with his long hair and scruffy beard, raised a hand. He appeared to be relaxed, draped over a chair, but Layne knew it was just for show. Instead, he made her think of a predator, ready to explode in a fighting rage at any moment. If she had to pick one word to describe him, it was wild. He looked like he should be living in an isolated cabin, wrestling bears or wolves, or something else with sharp teeth.

"This is Hale Carter. Man is a genius with anything with an engine or electronics. You need something fixed, he's your man."

"Nice to meet you." Hale's smile was wide and charismatic. "Sorry to hear you got hurt."

"Thank you." A bit of a charmer, this one. He had a handsome face and dark brown eyes, along with broad shoulders and muscled arms. She was sure he was as deadly as the rest of them.

"And this is Morgan Kincaid."

Layne nodded at the woman and she returned the gesture. She was seated, cleaning a hand gun on the table in front of her. From her moves, it looked like she'd done it many times before. The woman looked like she had tough and badass down to a fine art.

"Well, I welcome all the help you're bringing to keep my dig safe," she said.

Declan shifted. "That's not what you told me. You started bitching about us getting in your way."

"That was because you were being a pain. Issuing orders and getting all bossy."

Declan's gray eyes darkened and Layne heard Morgan snort.

"She's already got your number, boss man," Morgan said.

Declan pinched the bridge of his nose. "Okay, everyone strap in. We're about to take off."

Layne settled in her seat. Before she could do anything, Declan dropped down beside her and reached over and fastened her belt.

Even though they'd been pressed together already once before, this time, she was able to get the scent of him. Man with a hint of perspiration. Something told her Declan Ward didn't bother with fancy colognes. Warmth poured off his hard chest.

His fingers brushed her belly and she felt a tingle of heat. She sucked in a breath. His eyes whipped up to hers.

Shit. He felt it, too.

"I can do my own belt up, Ward."

"Your safety is my number-one concern now, Rush. Just doing my job." He sat back in his chair.

Layne's stomach did a funny flip-flop. She'd lost her parents when she'd been in her teens. Since then, she'd only had herself to depend on. No one else had ever worried about her safety.

He's getting paid for it, Layne. Don't get mushy. She looked away from him and felt the rumble of the jet's engines.

A man was not in her plan. Evan had made her swear off men for a few years. She had more to achieve in her career, more adventures to go on, and then she'd think about finding the right man.

Plus, she owed it to her parents to do the best she could in her career.

It was the two people who'd created her who'd stirred and fed her love of history. As an only child, she'd been a little spoiled, but not by things, instead by the unconditional love and attention from her parents. They'd been poor by most standards, but she'd never felt the lack growing up. Her father had spent every Sunday afternoon snuggled up with her watching history documentaries. Her mother had taken her to museums every month.

They'd been the best family, despite having cheap clothes and no fancy things, until the day it had all come crashing down.

She owed them. And Declan Ward, for all his dark, sexy looks, was not the right man for her.

***

"I hate the desert."

Dec turned, his boots sinking into the golden sand of the dune, and eyed Logan as his friend joined him. "You've sure spent a hell of a lot of time in them, O'Connor."

Logan crossed his arms. "Well, when I joined the *Navy*, I didn't expect fucking sand all the fucking time. It itches, it's scratchy, and it gets into places where you really don't want it. Now that I'm not a SEAL anymore, I was hoping for no sand."

"Quit your bitching," Dec said. "You're being paid far better than the Navy ever paid you."

Logan let out a gusty sigh. "That is true."

Dec let his gaze drift over the archeological dig. They were deep into the Western Desert, and the sun was bright and hot in the clear blue sky.

Local laborers were hard at work, moving buckets of sand and lowering ropes into the large hole in the ground. Many were dressed in the lightweight jellabiya robes. Here and there, it was easy to spot the archeologists and their student assistants. They were all wearing wide-brimmed hats, and light-colored trousers and shirts.

They'd been here a day, and Dec and his team had already finished their assessment and started implementing new security procedures. The security guards they were working with were local but trained by an international security company. Not the best Dec had worked with, but not the worst.

There'd been no sign of Anders, and Dec wasn't sure whether to be grateful or worried.

The one person who wasn't making it easy was a certain archeologist.

He spotted a slim figure talking earnestly with some of the local workers. Rush tended to speak with her hands, and she rivaled an admiral at giving out orders. She always seemed to be busy doing something. He suspected relaxing was not in her vocabulary.

They'd butted heads. A few times.

As he watched, she smiled at the workers, then moved out onto the wooden scaffold that lined one side of the deep excavation. She disappeared from view.

A light wind picked up, throwing sand Dec's way. He saw Hale circle around some tents and head up the dune toward Dec and Logan.

"Hate the sand," Hale grumbled.

Dec grunted and thrust a thumb at Logan. "Join Logan's club."

"Kind of jealous that your brother scored the other job," Hale said.

Dec wasn't so sure Callum would agree. "Cal's in the jungle. You have sand, he has mosquitos."

"I hate mosquitos," Logan added.

"I think you're both going soft on me." Dec looked at Hale. "Safe all set up?"

The man nodded. "Yep. Left a few artifacts in the storage tent, but that gold dog and anything else valuable will go in the safe I have hidden in one of the personal tents."

"Good work." A rush of movement around the excavation made Dec focus back on the dig. He frowned, wondering what was going on.

"Dr. Rush is planning to bring up a stone statue. A big sucker," Logan said. "She's pretty excited about a big lump of rock."

The workers were tossing ropes down into the hole.

"Better keep an eye on this." Dec started down the hill. "Hale, check out the western side of the site and check in with the guards."

"Got it."

"Logan, check in with Morgan. I want to make

sure we haven't seen any signs of anyone trying to get close to this dig."

Logan nodded. "On it."

In an instant, Logan and Hale turned into the serious former soldiers they were.

Dec reached the excavation hole and saw the workers heaving back on the ropes. He could hear Rush yelling orders up from the bottom of the pit. He stayed to the side, scanning, making sure everything was okay.

Then he heard a *thwap* sound. Workers started shouting.

A rope had snapped.

The workers on the other rope were pulled toward the hole.

Dec touched his earpiece, sprinting forward. "Logan, we need another rope. Fast."

Dec jumped over the scaffold railing, landing on the uppermost wooden platform. He saw the large statue of a man hanging at a precarious angle. Below, Rush was urging workers and archeologists to get out of the way.

Then he heard another sound.

A metallic ping.

The scaffold beneath his feet lurched away from the wall.

Shit. The screws had given way and the scaffold was threatening to collapse.

He spread his feet, trying to balance on the wobbling structure. Below, he heard panicked cries. Workers stuck on the scaffold were trying to get down, making it rock even more.

"Dec!"

Logan's and Morgan's heads appeared above. Logan tossed a coiled rope down.

Dec grabbed the rope, moving it through his hands, getting a feel for the weight of it. He quickly made a loop at the end, then he leaned over, eyeing the dangling carving.

Then he saw Rush, right below the statue, helping workers down off the scaffold.

His jaw tightened, but he forced himself to judge the distance to the dangling artifact and compensate for the sway of the scaffold.

He tossed the rope.

The loop fell perfectly over the end of the statue. He pulled back, tightening the rope.

"Logan?"

"Here."

Dec tossed the rope up. Logan grabbed it and yanked.

The statue leveled out and moved upward.

Dec swung onto the outside of the scaffold and quickly climbed down. He felt the structure tilt farther away from the wall. He moved faster.

It was going to come crashing down at any second.

He felt more screws let go, felt the wood giving way.

Dec leaped the last few feet to the ground, rolling once, then coming back up on his feet. He saw Rush and two workers still in the line of fire.

"Run!" he called out in Arabic. The workers scrambled back toward where the others were huddled by the far wall.

"The artifacts—" Rush's face was pale, her eyes wide.

Dec ran like a football linebacker. He scooped Rush off her feet, hearing her muffled cry. He heard the groan of the structure falling behind them.

Then he swung her around in his arms and skidded toward the far wall like a baseball player into home base, keeping her tucked tight against his chest.

The scaffold slammed into the ground behind them, and a cloud of dust rose up.

He sat up and Rush did, too. She was coughing, waving her hand to clear the air.

"What the hell did you think you were doing?" he bit out.

***

Layne coughed one more time, enjoying the feel of a hard, muscled chest pressed up against her.

Pity the muscles belonged to an awfully cranky, bossy man.

She straightened, pulling away from him. She'd been working on isolated digs her entire career. Not to mention the halls of academia. She was used to cranky men. She'd dealt with crankier.

"Well—"

"You have a damned artifact dangling precariously and it weighs a hell of a lot more than you, and a scaffold threatening to collapse, so you decided to stand right under it?"

She straightened at his cutting tone. "I was helping my people get to safety. I was trying to see if I could save any artifacts. My people, my dig, Declan."

And Layne intended for the rest of this dig to go off without a hitch. She eyed the shattered remains of the scaffold. Her chest tightened. Well, no more hitches.

Declan pushed to his feet in one lithe flex of muscle.

Layne quickly stood, not wanting to have him towering over her.

Not that it helped. She was average height, and he was well north of six feet. Even with his khaki cargo trousers and shirt covered in dust, the man made an impact. She hated that she kept noticing that—the muscled body, the lean face, the intense gray eyes.

"You do not risk your life." His face hardened. "My company was hired to take the risks. We take care of security, and the lives of the people on this dig."

"I'm not going to sit around watching and wringing my hands like some medieval damsel."

Declan thrust his hands on his hips. "Rush—"

Ugh. She hated when he said her name in that tone. She turned away. "I need to check the statue."

Firm fingers circled her arm and she felt his touch burning through her shirt.

"The scaffold is in pieces. You can't get out yet."

Dammit, he was right. "I need to check my team, as well."

He eyed her for a second. "The statue made it out okay. Logan has it secured at the top."

Relief punched through her and she forced herself to be polite. "Thank you."

A brief smile flickered over Declan's face. "That didn't hurt too much, did it?"

She shook her arm free of his hold. "It stung a little."

His smile widened, but when he touched his ear, she realized his team was contacting him.

Layne took the chance to head over to where her archeologists and grad students sat huddled with the local workers. "Everyone okay?"

There were nods and grumbles. She was damn grateful that no one was injured.

"Dr. Rush, we could have been killed. I am extremely upset this occurred, and want to know how you'll ensure this doesn't happen again."

Layne rolled her eyes at the snippy voice. She turned and faced her senior archeologist, Dr. Aaron Stiller. Almost every day, she regretted choosing him as part of the team. She knew he had been hoping to land the job as head of this dig, and had been disappointed he'd lost out to her.

He'd been taking that disappointment out on her daily.

"Dr. Stiller, I will ensure this is investigated."

Stiller was in his forties, tall and very thin, with a head that was rapidly losing its hair. The man sniffed. "All the work we've done down here is ruined."

She turned and eyed their worksite. The carefully placed markers and ropes were all jumbled. She saw several pots had been smashed. She sighed. There was nothing of huge monetary value damaged, but it still hurt her heart a bit. Everything they dug up was a piece of history and that made it valuable to her.

"Rush?"

Declan's voice made her turn.

He waved to a rope ladder that had been dropped into the excavation. It was what they'd used before the scaffold had been erected.

"Okay, everyone," she said, clapping her hands. "Let's get topside and take a break."

She watched her team all head up the ladder.

Then she felt a hand touch her side. She gasped, grabbing the thick wrist.

"You're bleeding." Declan was frowning. He tugged at her shirt.

"Hey." She slapped at his hands.

"There's blood on your shirt. Let me see."

"It's nothing." Now that he mentioned it, she felt a slight sting.

He tugged her shirt free from her cargo trousers and lifted the hem a few inches.

Layne huffed out a breath. She'd been looking after herself a very, very long time. She wasn't used to anyone tending her wounds but herself. She felt the stroke of callused fingers on the skin of her belly and her breath rushed out.

"Scratch. Must have hit a rock." Declan was looking down, completely focused on her injury.

Layne blinked, pushing back the strange and unwanted warmth running through her. "It's nothing."

"Here." He pulled something from one of the million pockets on his cargo trousers. Then he pressed it to the scratch.

She blinked. It was a pink bandage with cartoon princesses on it. A reluctant laugh broke from her. "Why do you have kiddie bandages in your pocket?"

He grinned. "I get them for my guys. Logan hates them."

She shook her head and for a second, tried to imagine the intense and slightly scary Logan O'Connor wearing a pink bandage. She couldn't do it.

Her gaze settled back on Declan's dark head. She was amazed they weren't arguing. Since they'd reached the dig, he'd been busy trying to boss her around—security this and security that. Most of the things she'd agreed with—like the emergency backpacks everyone now had stowed in their tents. They contained rations, water and gear for surviving the desert. But some of the rules got in the way of them doing their job. No one was allowed to work alone, and no night digging. She wrinkled her nose. It was really going to slow down their progress.

She cleared her throat and stepped back. She shifted her gaze away from him, and that was when she saw it.

A huge, gaping hole in the side wall.

"Oh, my God." She hurried over and heard Declan mutter under his breath.

He grabbed her arm. "Where the hell are—"

"Declan, look."

He spotted the hole and stilled. "The scaffold must have knocked through the wall." He touched his ear. "Logan, Rush and I are taking a look around. Be up shortly."

"Come on." She patted her belt. "Dammit, I don't have my flashlight."

A bright beam of light clicked on. She eyed the large, rugged flashlight Declan held. It was nothing like her small, serviceable one.

Together, they approached the opening.

"Stay near me," he said. "I need to assess the stability—"

"I've done this a time or two, Ward."

She thought she heard him making a growling sound. "Just stay back and listen to me."

"How about I stay right beside you and we listen to each other?"

"You don't mind saying exactly what you think, do you, Rush?"

"Life's too short to beat around the bush."

Now she thought she heard him mutter something about stubborn mules and smart women. She grinned to herself.

As they neared the ragged hole, her heartbeat picked up. This was one of those moments that made all the long monotony of brushing away sand and dirt, of cataloguing every tiny shard of pottery, and spending hours soaking and cleaning artifacts worthwhile.

These once-in-a-lifetime moments were the ones she'd dreamed about as a little girl. Layne stopped and waited while Declan shone the flashlight around inside.

"Holy hell," he muttered.

Layne swallowed her giddy excitement.

It was another room and it was richly decorated with art. Declan's light illuminated the barely faded reds, golds, and blues.

"It's the main burial chamber," she whispered. "I *knew* it was here."

The walls went dark as the light moved and she realized he was studying the roof.

"Looks sturdy," he said.

"Good." She slipped in before he could stop her.

"*Dammit*, Rush."

"It looks New Kingdom, maybe Third Intermediate Period." She saw an image of everyday life, women in flowing white gowns, one breast exposed. A beautiful temple by the banks of an oasis. A man in the typical rigid pose, one foot forward and holding a jar. "This is really high quality. Whoever is buried here was someone important."

"This really gets you going, huh?"

She turned and saw Declan studying her like she was a strange specimen under a microscope.

"Come on, you're telling me none of this excites you? She held her hands out. "Standing in a place no living soul has been in for thousands of years? A chance to uncover a fascinating piece of history?"

He raised one brow. "Maybe a little. Watching you do it is pretty exciting."

Her heart tripped. If he hadn't said it so matter-of-factly, she would have accused him of flirting. Not that she guessed Declan Ward ever flirted. Hell, the man didn't need to, not when he exuded that sexy, dangerous aura that would draw women like bees to honey.

She cleared her throat. "Let's look at the back—"

Declan swiveled the light and Layne gasped. Her stomach tightened. "A sarcophagus."

A huge stone box made of granite stood on a raised platform. Above it, the roof had been carved in an arch and painted blue. It was dotted with gold stars and a woman's long outstretched body.

"She's Nut, right?" he said.

Layne nodded. "Goddess of the Sky and mother of Seth. She was often painted on the vaults of tombs and inside the lid of a sarcophagus. She protected the dead."

Then Layne spotted the artwork on the back wall behind the sarcophagus. "Wow." She'd never seen anything like it.

It was a painting of a huge, dog-like animal. Wild and fierce, it had a straight, forked tail and triangular ears. It was like it was posed over the sarcophagus, also protecting whoever rested inside.

"Looks like the set-animal," Declan said. "Looks like whoever was buried here didn't buy into the bad stuff about Seth."

"No." She moved closer to the sarcophagus. "If

this is from the New Kingdom period, it makes sense. There was a resurgence of support for Seth, led by the great pharaohs Seti and Rameses II."

She touched the smooth granite of the burial box, wondering at the long-ago artisan who'd toiled to make it.

Who was buried inside?

"Hey, the lid's broken off in the corner," Declan said.

Layne frowned. "Dammit. Probably means grave robbers beat us here by a few thousand years." She shot him a sour look. "Perhaps Hasan's ancestors."

Declan looked around. "Doesn't look like it's been disturbed. Could they have broken the lid when they put it here?"

"Possibly. Maybe they didn't have time to replace it. Plus out here, we're really far from the source of granite used to create this." She pushed up, trying to see into the hole. She saw nothing but black shadows.

"Here." Declan moved, and his front pressed up against her back, trapping her against the stone.

God, the man was as hard as the granite. Her pulse tripped and she tried to tell herself it was the excitement of the find. Nothing to do with her annoying, sexy security specialist.

He angled the light to shine into the hole.

"I can't see anything. I'm not tall enough."

Hands gripped her waist and before she could say anything, he boosted her up.

Layne rested her hands on the stone, excruciatingly conscious of Declan behind her, around her. Blindly, she focused on the sarcophagus. When she saw what was inside, she went rigid.

Declan leaned over her shoulder.

"Damn," he breathed, his breath brushing her ear.

The inner sarcophagus glinted...with gold.

Chapter Five

Dec stared at the glittering color visible through the hole.

"The inner sarcophagus is made entirely of gold," Rush breathed. "Oh, my God, Declan, this is huge!"

She spun in his arms, energy and excitement radiating off her. Her thighs clamped onto his hips and her jubilant laugh raced over him, making his gut clench.

Then she leaned forward and smacked her lips to his. It was only a second, and then she pulled back and laughed again.

Dec blinked, trying to calm the growing roar in his head. It was the sound of a hungry beast, and it wanted more of Dr. Layne Rush.

"Declan?" Her laugh died, her gaze glued to his face in the light of his flashlight. "Sorry. Blame that kiss on the excitement."

"I don't think so."

She blinked. "What?"

"Let's try it again, to test your theory."

Her eyes widened, and this time, it was Dec who pressed his mouth to hers.

For a second, she stiffened in his arms. He

moved his lips, learned the feel of hers, getting that tantalizing taste of her.

Then she moaned. Her hands slid into his hair and she kissed him back.

Damn. Desire slammed into Dec like a bullet at close range. He pulled her closer and opened her lips with his tongue. Then her tongue was there, sliding along his.

He thrust deep, tilting her head back. She moaned, her hands tugging on his hair. She kissed him back with an intensity that sucked his breath away. He cupped the firm globes of her ass, pulling her even closer. She was the perfect armful of toned curves.

"Dec, you copy? Dec, if you don't fucking answer me in the next three seconds, I'm coming down there with the cavalry."

Logan's voice echoed in Dec's desire-fuzzed mind.

He pulled back, heard Layne's little cry of protest. His chest was heaving and so was hers. She raised a shaky hand and pushed the hair back from her face.

"Well..." She looked down and when she realized he'd rested her on the edge of the outer stone sarcophagus, her eyes widened. "Oh my God, let me down. I could damage this."

He gripped her waist with one hand and helped her down. He touched his ear with the other hand. "I copy, Logan. We're fine. Made a discovery. We'll be up in a minute."

Layne was watching him. "We can't go up now, I

have too much work to do—"

"Sun will be setting soon, Rush."

"Dammit, can't you relax the rules?"

"No. Anders attacked you at night. You need the right equipment down here, and besides, I need time to work out how to contain the news of this find. Because once it gets out—"

"Anders will be back." Her face paled a little. "Okay, so for now, we keep it quiet."

He nodded. "Logan and I will watch the excavation site tonight."

She tossed her head back, rubbing at a streak of dust on her cheek. "What happened before…"

Dec, still feeling the edge of desire riding him hard, cocked his head. "What was that?"

"Oh, don't make this difficult, Declan."

"You mean that moment when you had your hands clamped in my hair, your legs wrapped around my hips, and your tongue down my throat?"

She hissed out a breath. "You are so infuriating sometimes. The kiss."

He leaned in close, his nose brushing hers. "That was more than a kiss, Rush."

Her gaze dropped and he knew she couldn't miss his erection straining against his pants. She jerked her eyes up.

"Adrenaline, excitement…look, it isn't going to happen again." She shook her head. "It was a lapse. You have a job to do, and I have a job to do."

Yeah, she had a point. And Dec didn't mess around with women like Layne. She was made for the whole shebang—career, family, kids. All the stuff Dec knew he couldn't do. All the stuff he knew he didn't deserve.

"You got it, Rush. Let's write it off as temporary insanity." His gut turned over. Damn, he hated just saying the words.

He expected to see relief on her face, but some other strange mix of emotions crossed her features. "Good. Right."

"Now let's get out of here, before Logan storms in looking to rescue us."

She pressed her palm to the stone. "I can't wait to get back here tomorrow."

A loud click echoed in the tomb. Dec tensed. When he saw the stone lid of the sarcophagus start to retract, he quickly pulled Layne closer to him.

"What the hell?" She watched, mouth open, as the entire lid disappeared into the wall. "I've never seen or heard of anything like this before. There must be some sort of mechanism—"

They both peered over the edge.

The smaller golden sarcophagus inside was shaped vaguely like a man. The bottom half of it was smooth but covered in hieroglyphs. A large, elaborate necklace covered the chest, and it was decorated in layers of bright-blue, semi-precious stone, and another translucent stone of startling gold-yellow color. In the center was a huge, oval-shaped pendant in the same gold stone.

The face on the sarcophagus wasn't human. It looked like a dog.

"Set-animal again?" Dec asked.

Layne was staring at the artifact, drinking in all

the details. "Maybe. It could be Anubis. He was also depicted with a canine head, and was the god of mummification and the afterlife." She pulled some thin gloves out of her pocket and pulled them on. Then she reached over to touch the stone amulet in the center of the chest.

"I've never seen a rock that color," Dec said.

"It...my God, I think it's Libyan desert glass."

"Which is?"

She looked over her shoulder. "A mysterious yellow glass found strewn across a portion of the Western Desert bordering Libya. It's suspected it was created when a meteor crashed into the sand. King Tutankhamun had some of this in his treasures, but it was a long and dangerous journey to collect it."

"Western Desert again." Everything seemed to be pointing in one direction.

She touched the desert glass again before she snatched her hand back. "Oh."

The yellow glass started to sink into the sarcophagus.

Suddenly, the chest of the sarcophagus started to open.

"My God. I've never seen anything like this," Rush said. "Oh, no, what if the mummy is exposed?" Panic filled her voice. "It'll deteriorate."

The chest plates opened out, like petals on a flower. But no bandage-wrapped mummy was below. "Looks like it's only a compartment in the gold. It doesn't go all the way through," he said.

And inside the space rested a small gold cylinder.

"God." Rush reached in and carefully lifted the artifact out. "It's a scroll. Made entirely of gold!"

"I've heard of the Copper Scroll," Declan said. "But not a gold scroll."

It was only as long as her palm, but perfectly formed. It was made with small hinges and they easily rolled out.

It was filled with hieroglyphs.

"I can't leave it here," she said.

"Got something to wrap it in?"

She nodded. "I have a pack in the main excavation area."

"I'll get it."

Dec was back moments later with a backpack. Carefully, Layne lifted the scroll and together they settled it into the bag.

The shadows had really thickened and Dec knew that above, the sun would be setting soon. "All right, Rush, we keep the scroll between you and me and my team. Got it?"

She nodded.

"Good. Now, let's get out of here."

"The sarcophagus—?"

"I'll work out how to close it up and don't worry, my team and I will keep an eye on it tonight."

They left the tomb and crossed over to the rope ladder. He gestured for her to go first. She planted a boot on the bottom rung and grabbed another one with her hand.

Then she paused. "Declan—"

His gaze met hers and for a beat, they stared at each other.

He wasn't sure who moved first, her or him, but she was back in his arms, the kiss hot and just a little wild.

When she pulled back, she licked her lips, her gaze a little dazed.

Shit. Layne Rush was going to be a problem. One he knew he should steer clear of, but wasn't going to.

"Climb the ladder, Rush."

"Ladder. Right." She grabbed the rope rung and climbed. Dec followed her up, and every time he glanced upward he was rewarded with a view of her spectacular ass flexing under her cargo trousers.

He drew in a breath.

She reached the top and pulled herself over. Dec cleared the last few rungs and climbed out. His team was waiting at the top.

"Nice of you to join us," Logan drawled.

Dec barely resisted giving his friend the finger. "We need to talk." Subtly, Dec tipped his head toward the hole. "Some new finds will need securing."

Logan's eyes widened a fraction. "Sure thing." The man turned to Layne. "Doc, we've put the statue in the work tent."

"The statue?"

Logan raised a brow. "Yeah, the stone one you were so excited about. The one that almost dropped on your head."

"Oh, right." She shook her head. "Right. I'll take a look at it." Then her shoulders sagged. "First, I need to deal with the scaffold mess—"

"Go, Rush."

She glanced up at Declan.

"Go." Dec jerked his head toward the work tent. He knew she was dying to get her hands on the scroll nestled in the bag on her shoulder. "I'll deal with the scaffold."

She looked torn. "You're sure?"

His lips quirked. "You'll have to thank me again."

That snapped her spine straight, and for a second he thought she was going to be stubborn and decide to deal with the scaffold anyway.

Declan shook his head. "You know what? I'll let you off this time."

"Doc?" Piper Ross hurried over, followed by some other members of the team.

"Dr. Rush, the statue is amazing," a young man said, waving his hands. "You need to see it."

As her archeologists reached her, she shared one last look with Declan, then she turned and followed her team.

"You want to tell me what really happened down there?" Logan said, once Layne was out of earshot.

"Yeah. We found a tomb. Paintings, artifacts...and a gold sarcophagus. And a secret golden scroll."

"Shit." Logan stepped in front of him. "And you going to tell me why your hair is all messed up, and the lovely doctor had swollen lips like someone just kissed the hell out of her?"

Dec straightened, and saw Hale and Morgan grinning at him. "No idea what you're talking about."

Logan just raised a brow at him.

Dec turned away. "Come on, O'Connor. Instead of gossiping, how about we get to work?"

***

The sun was setting, turning the desert sands gold, orange, and red.

Dec stood near the edge of the camp, staring out at the sunset.

He figured the beautiful view should make his breath catch, or make him feel...something. Instead, he didn't feel much at all.

He rubbed his belly, feeling the thick ridge of scar tissue through the cotton of his shirt. He'd gotten out, he'd survived. He had friends, family, and a really good business. One he enjoyed.

He should quit worrying because a sunset didn't excite him.

Besides, one thing had really excited him—kissing Layne Rush.

Dec closed his eyes. God, he had work to do. He didn't need a super-smart, opinionated woman messing him up. And she certainly didn't need a man like him messing up her life. She had no idea what he was truly capable of.

As he turned to face the darkening camp, his jaw tightened.

The local workers were all gathered around a fire, talking quietly and drinking what they called coffee. The stuff tasted like dirt and twigs to him, so he steered clear of it.

What was worrying him was his and Logan's analysis of the scaffold. He'd spent a couple of hours down in the excavation with Logan, cleaning it up and helping the workers put the scaffold back together.

He had nothing definitive, but there were small signs that said its collapse hadn't been an accident.

The scratch marks on the anchor points, the loose and worn bolts. It could just be a coincidence, but Dec wasn't really one for hoping things were just a quirk of fate. Too many times on a mission with his SEAL team, he'd seen that coincidence turn into a big pile of shit.

It paid to gather information, plan and be ready, just in case coincidence turned out to be someone with a hard-on for making your day suck.

Dec touched his earpiece. "Logan? Everything quiet?"

"As a graveyard," Logan replied.

"This is technically a graveyard." Dec's dark thoughts went back to the collapsed scaffold. He could picture Layne standing there, about to be crushed. "Let's just keep it an ancient one, not a modern-day one."

"Boogeyman getting to you, Dec?" Morgan's voice.

"The scaffold incident has left me cautious."

Logan's snort came clearly through the line.

"You're always cautious. Cautious is your middle name."

"Just keep an eye out, okay?"

"Always do."

Dec circled the camp. He checked the smaller personal tents. Most were dark, everyone exhausted from a busy day. One or two had faint lights on inside. The archeologists reading up or planning for the next day.

Then he spotted the larger storage and work tents.

One still had lights burning bright.

He knew who was up and working.

The canvas flap of the doorway was rolled up and tied. He stood there for a second, watching her.

She wasn't hard to watch. She was bent over a makeshift wooden bench. On top of it lay the golden scroll from the sarcophagus. She wasn't wearing her hat now, and her rich, dark hair fell around her shoulders.

She was wearing gloves and touching the scroll like it was the most precious thing she'd ever seen. The look on her face...it trapped his gaze. He stepped closer, trying to see exactly what she was looking at. She grabbed a pen and scratched some notes down in the notebook at her elbow.

Then she straightened like she'd been shot and spun toward him. She led with her fist, her green-gold eyes wide, her body tensed.

Not expecting the move at all, her fist slammed into his face.

"Goddammit." He staggered backward, grabbing

his nose. "What the hell, Rush?"

The air rushed out of her. "Dammit, Declan, you scared me."

"So you thought you'd punch me?"

"I thought you were an attacker." She bit down on her lip, looking like she was trying not to laugh.

"It hurts," he said with a burst of annoyance.

Now she did laugh. "I know. I'm sorry."

He probed it gently. "Don't think you broke it."

She looked contrite now. "It's been broken before."

"Yeah, my brother Callum slugged me in the face when we were kids. My father grounded him and my mother told me to move quicker next time."

Layne's lips twitched. "Should I get you some ice?"

"I'm fine."

"God, you move quietly. You really did scare me."

"Sorry. My training. And nothing to do with the fact that you were completely absorbed in your work."

She tilted her head. "They teach you to be super quiet in security school?"

Damn, she could be a smart aleck. "No, in SEAL training. You need to pay more attention to your surroundings, Rush."

"I will."

He snorted, not buying her contrite tone for a second. "Is your hand okay?"

She flexed it. "I'll survive."

"So, how's the work going?" he asked.

"Okay." Her nose screwed up in an adorable fashion. "I've been working to translate the hieroglyphs etched on the scroll." She lifted a magnifying glass over the golden surface.

Dec studied the symbols.

"The occupant of the tomb is Itennu. He was a high-ranking priest of Seth, and he commissioned this scroll. I haven't finished deciphering all of it yet. I'll be honest, most of it just doesn't make sense." She sighed. "I think I'm missing something. Added to that, some of the hieroglyphs are a little unusual, so it's taking me some time to translate them. This one here has me stumped—" She pointed to a tiny squiggle. "I'm going to need to pull my books and tablet out..." She drifted off. "I'm boring you."

"Not at all. We might not see eye-to-eye on running all aspects of this dig, Rush, but I admire your excitement and enthusiasm for your work."

She was staring at him like he'd shocked her. Her gaze ran over his face. He felt much like the antiquities under her hands. A puzzle for her to decode.

He leaned closer, feeling her shoulder brush his side. "What's this?"

There were some strange grooves in the center of the scroll where there were no hieroglyphs, except for that strange symbol she'd pointed at.

"I'm honestly not sure. It doesn't look familiar."

"You'll work it out." He turned his head, and she was watching him. Damn, his gut went hard. "Rush, keep looking at me like that and I'm going to kiss you again."

She licked her lips and Dec swallowed a groan.

"I won't deny I'm attracted to you," she said. "But we have a business arrangement, Declan. And I don't have time for a man like you."

"A man like me?"

She waved a hand. "Sexy, potent, attractive." When Declan grinned she rolled her eyes. "This dig has gotten off to a bad start. I need to ensure it goes smoothly from here. I'm sure the sex would be great…"

"Great? Rush, I assure you, it would be something well above *great.*"

That made her pause, a flush of color in her cheeks. "I've never really experienced anything above good."

Dec made a pained sound. Oh, he wanted to strip her naked and show her just how amazing it could be. "That makes me want you more, not less. But you have a point."

She blinked. "I do?"

He reached out and fiddled with the buttons on her shirt. "I'm not the man for you. I don't do relationships. I'm not a forever kind of guy." Jesus, for the first time in his life, he seriously regretted that. "You need someone better than me." He held out his hands. "I've done too much, seen too much—" Dec broke off. Hell, he'd never told any woman anything like this before.

Rush cocked her hip. "You're too big and bad for me, is that it?"

"Yes," he said warily, her tone setting off

warning bells in his head.

"Oh, I'm too innocent, sheltered, and naïve?"

"Ah...that's not what I said."

She shook her head at him. "You have no idea what I've lived through or experienced. We've all suffered horrible things, Declan. It doesn't give you a free pass to cut yourself off from life." She waved an angry hand. "Why don't you just head off and brood in the shadows for a bit, Ward. Maybe find yourself a Batcave. I have work to do."

When she gave him her back and turned her attention to the scroll, Dec just stared. What horrible things had Layne lived through? What made her voice quiver and her face go pale like that?

"Are you still here?" she asked.

Damn, this woman just loved busting his balls. "Someone will keep an eye on your work tent until you're finished." He didn't tell her he'd shifted the schedule around to make sure he was the one watching her tent. "When you're done, radio for one of us to walk you back to your tent. Got it?"

She didn't even look at him. "Got it."

Dec cleared his throat. He needed some distance between him and the lovely Dr. Rush. "Don't stay up too late, and that hieroglyph you can't decipher..."

She lifted her head.

"It stands for fierce protector." With that, Dec exited the tent.

Chapter Six

The next morning, Layne stomped across the dig site, tucking her shirt into her trousers as she went.

She'd slept in. She knew she shouldn't be angry at herself, as she'd stayed up way too late working on the scroll and then dreamed about a certain annoying, hard-bodied man, but she'd slept through her alarm and she hated being late.

After she'd gotten back to her tent the night before, escorted by the near-silent and intimidating Morgan, it had taken Layne a long time to fall asleep. Then she'd had strange dreams of golden sarcophagi and scrolls, and running through the desert dunes...then the dream had morphed into something else.

The sexy feel of a certain man's hands and lips. Declan slowly stripping her naked, his stubble scraping her belly and thighs, her husky cries. She'd woken up with damp panties.

Ugh, why was she thinking about Declan? Mr. I'm-too-dark-and-brooding-for-you. God, he'd gotten her all twisted up inside.

He had been right about the obscure hieroglyph, though. It did mean fierce protector. But no matter how she arranged what she'd decoded on the scroll, none of it made sense.

And just how the hell did a former Navy SEAL-turned-security specialist know how to read hieroglyphs, anyway? She wasn't buying that bull about 'absorbing' it on the job.

"Dr. Rush, nice to see you finally made an appearance."

She barely stopped herself from groaning aloud. She did not have the time or the patience for Dr. Stiller and his attitude this morning.

"Morning to you, too, Aaron. What do you want?"

He looked affronted. "I want to know what the hell you are going to do about all this? To ensure our safety. Someone sabotaged the scaffold and nearly killed us! The local workers are starting to whisper about a curse, what with your attack and the theft, and now this."

She froze. "Sabotaged the scaffold?"

A smug look crossed the man's face. "Yes. Mr. Ward informed us that the scaffold was intentionally made to fall and told us to check all equipment for any signs of tampering."

And Declan hadn't told her. She dragged in a deep breath. "Declan and his team are the security experts. We follow their recommendations." God, she needed some coffee. Or just some Diet Coke mainlined into her veins.

She spotted Declan watching a few of her team working a new area of excavation on the surface. Her guys were carefully dusting away sand from the large stone blocks.

She stomped up to him. "I need a word with you."

She saw Piper and two of her students look up. Yeah, they knew that tone meant she was on the warpath.

Declan didn't appear concerned.

"Fine." He led her a little away from her team. "How are you feeling this morning?"

"I'm tired and cranky."

He raised a brow. "What's got your panties in a twist?"

That just made her blood fire more. "My panties are not up for discussion. What is going to be discussed is that you think the scaffold was tampered with and I'm only just hearing about it this morning, from my senior archeologist."

Declan sighed. "Stiller, right? I asked him to keep it quiet until I spoke with you. I wanted to finish gathering evidence first, not come to you with half-baked theories. I was checking out the scaffold again this morning, and Stiller asked what I was doing. I didn't think I needed to keep it a secret before updating you. I'd planned to talk to you this morning, but you were getting some much needed sleep."

She lifted her hat and resettled it on her head. "Okay, sorry if I jumped all over you."

Those fine lips twitched again. "You keep this up, I'll lose track of the number of apologies I have from you."

"Ward, tell me about the scaffold." Or she was going to hit him.

He nodded. "Definite marks that it was tampered with. But someone put a lot of effort into making it look like it happened all by itself."

A cold shiver went through her. "Why?"

"My guess? They wanted an accident to happen that might cause the dig to be cancelled, or at least put on hold. Everyone leaves the site…"

"And Anders and his black-market looters move in," she said grimly. "No one is getting *anything* from this dig." She chewed it all over. "So someone snuck in and did this?"

Declan's gaze narrowed. "I don't think so. I think it was an inside job."

She hissed out a breath. "No."

"Maybe one of your archeologists—"

She shook her head. "No. I know them all personally, hand-picked them for the team. None of them could do this."

"Dr. Stiller?"

Layne shook her head. "We don't see eye-to-eye, but I can't see him doing anything to jeopardize the dig."

"Even if it means casting you in a poor light and gaining the top job for himself?"

"God, are you always so cynical?"

"Yep. I'm a realist."

She eyed him for a second, the strong lines of his face and the shadows in his eyes. While she wasn't going to let him get away with using his past as a barrier, she had no doubt Declan had seen too much of the worst the world had to offer. She turned her thoughts to Dr. Stiller. "I wouldn't put it past Aaron to try to do something to get me removed, if the opportunity presented itself. But this? It's one step too far, even for him."

"Then the local workers."

She grimaced. "I don't know them all, but they all came recommended. And the ones I've been working with, well, they seem loyal, and they're hard, efficient workers."

"Rush, Anders and the people behind the black-market antiquities trade have deep pockets. If one of your people has a debt, a sick mother, or a family to feed…"

He left the thought hanging there and it dug into her skin. "Okay, so we keep an eye out. Make sure nothing like this can happen again."

"That's the plan."

She fiddled with her hat. "I don't understand how people can kill over this."

Declan's face hardened. "I've seen people kill for far less. Hell, I saw Anders kill just for the fun of it."

She stilled. "You saw Anders kill people?"

Declan muttered a soft curse, his face hardening. "I'm not going to let Anders get anywhere near you again."

God, the pain. It was buried deep in his voice, his eyes. Whatever had happened with Anders, it had left a lasting scar on Declan Ward. One he hadn't let heal. "I know. And I'm not going to let him take any more artifacts. They should be there for us to learn from, for everyone to see."

Declan shrugged. "The past is the past. Are they

really that important?"

Her blood fired. "Yes. We can learn so much from our ancestors, maybe even avoid past mistakes."

His gray eyes churned and chilled. "There have been wars in the past and in the present, and I'm pretty sure there will be wars in the future. I don't think we learn from hunks of pottery and gold statues, Rush."

There was that pain again, and it hurt her heart.

"We can," she said softly. "That's why I do my job, keep discovering, keep learning and keep trying to get the stories out there." She studied him. "How did you know what that hieroglyph was? It's an obscure variant, not known to many."

"My parents are pretty interested in Egyptian history."

"No history teacher would know this, Declan."

A faint smile on his lips. "My parents aren't history teachers. Well, I guess you could say my father is. He's a professor at Denver University."

The name clicked and Layne gasped. "Your father is Dr. Oliver Ward?"

Declan nodded. "And my mother is—"

"Persephone Ward." Shock filled Layne. She couldn't believe it.

Declan's smile widened. "Yeah, she's—"

"A treasure hunter," Layne said.

A rueful look crossed his face. "I prefer artifact acquisition specialist, but she prefers treasure hunter."

Layne couldn't believe one of the greatest teachers of ancient history was Declan's father, and one of the wildest, most daring treasure hunters was his mother. Declan neither screamed academic nor wild risk taker.

"They must have been shocked when you joined the Navy." And joined one of the toughest Special Forces teams in the world.

"At first. Then my brother, Callum, joined, too. They got used to it."

"Well, thanks to your help, I got most of the glyphs translated last night. Not that they make any sense." She frowned. "They seem disjointed, incomplete."

Declan straightened and touched his ear. "Logan needs me. I'll let you get back to your work. And Rush?"

"Yes?"

"Let me know before you move the gold sarcophagus. I want to make sure it's moved safely."

She watched him go. He moved with a controlled grace, a coiled strength that said he could explode into action at any moment.

She was glad Declan Ward was watching over her dig.

"Dr. Rush, I do not blame you for getting yourself an eyeful of that."

Layne turned and spotted Piper. "We just finished discussing some security business—"

"Uh-huh." Piper pulled a hard, grape-flavored candy out of her pocket, unwrapped it, and popped it in her mouth. "Yeah, I could see by the way you were watching the man's mighty fine ass that you were thinking of security business."

Layne pinched the bridge of her nose. Which she seemed to do a lot when she was talking with Piper. She liked the woman, but sometimes she made Layne want to take a painkiller and lie down.

Piper sucked loudly on her candy. "Sure is a shame I prefer girls, otherwise I'd give you a run for your money with that one, Doc."

Layne heaved out a breath. "Did you need me for something, Piper?"

"Yeah." Piper's cute face turned serious. "The workers are all pretty freaked out about everything."

Layne groaned. "Dr. Stiller mentioned a rumor of a curse is getting around."

"Yep. And a few of the workers and a couple of our team are sick this morning. Bad tummies and lots of trips to the toilets." Piper grimaced. "Since they're those horrible portable toilets, I'm guessing it isn't going to be pretty for the rest of us who need to go."

Things like this were common problems on a dig. "Upset stomachs are the norm in Egypt. We need to make sure everyone is drinking the bottled water provided."

"But the local workers as well?"

Now Layne frowned. Piper was right, the locals shouldn't be upset by the water or the food. "Okay, well it must have been something bad in the food last night. Pretty sure no mummies climbed out of the excavation to poison anyone. Come on, let's make sure everyone who's not feeling well is settled in their tents."

Piper nodded. "Guess that means the rest of us will have more work to do today."

"Yes. It does. But I have something that'll help lighten the load."

"Oh?" Piper looked intrigued.

"When the scaffold collapsed, it knocked a hole in the wall."

Piper straightened. "And?"

Layne grinned. "I found something."

"You're killing me here, Doc." Piper bounced on her feet. "What?"

"Wonderful things."

***

Dec dodged the punch.

He spun and kicked out, his foot connecting with a hard abdomen.

There was a grunt. "Easy, Dec."

Dec pulled back, bouncing on his feet in the sand. He and Logan had a bit of down time, so they were sparring. Logan was bigger and stronger, but Dec was faster. Besides, they'd been sparring for years now. They knew each other's strengths and weaknesses.

Dec came in low and managed a blow to Logan's side. The big man dodged away, cursing.

"Getting rusty, old man." Dec grinned.

Logan growled. "I'll show you old."

The next few blows were hard and fierce. It took everything Dec had to block them. Then, with a roar, Logan tackled him. They both landed hard on the ground.

"We'll call it a draw," Dec rasped, spitting out a mouthful of sand.

Logan flopped back in the sand, shading his face with an arm. "How long until we're on duty?"

"An hour. I'm sure Hale and Morgan are keen for a break by now." Dec drew his knees up. Even though he wasn't officially on duty, they were still sparring on Dec's favorite sand dune. The one that gave him a perfect view of the dig and surroundings.

Since the scaffold, there had been no problems. No sign of intruders. No sign of Anders.

Nothing.

It made Dec nervous and itchy. He much preferred action.

"You're on edge, my friend," Logan said.

Dec turned his head and saw Logan watching him. He shrugged. "Anders isn't really the patient type. I expected him to make a move before now." Especially since they'd brought the golden sarcophagus up. While he and Layne had kept the scroll under wraps, he was certain news of the sarcophagus would have reached Dakhla and beyond.

"Everything's quiet," Logan said. "We should be grateful."

"I know."

"Maybe it's not just the job getting to you.

Maybe it has something to do with a certain sexy, mouthy archeologist?"

Dec narrowed his gaze at his friend but stayed silent.

"Come on, Dec." Logan sat up. "I've seen the way you look at her. Watch her when she isn't looking. I haven't seen you look at anyone that way—"

"Drop it, O'Connor. There is nothing going on with Rush and me."

"Oh? In that case, you won't mind if I take a stab at her? That mouth of hers—"

Dec moved without thinking. He blinked and realized he had the front of Logan's shirt bunched in his hands.

His friend had a smug grin on his face.

"You're an asshole." Dec let him go.

"I like her," Logan said.

Shit. Dec ran his hands through his hair. He did, too. Too much. "I'm a one night kind of guy, that's all I have to offer. She's not." She deserved so much better.

"You don't have to be. I know you're dragging around all that stuff with Anders—"

Dec sliced a hand through the air. "Right now, all I can focus on is keeping her safe."

Logan raised a brow. "I thought you were focused on catching Anders."

Dec stilled. "That, too." But his gaze moved over the dig until he found the head covered by a battered hat, and the tight, compact body. She was hunched over, working with that fierce concentration of hers.

Dec had been after Anders for years. But he knew if it came down to Layne or Anders, Dec would protect her with his last breath.

"Dec, do you copy?"

Morgan's voice came through his earpiece. "Yeah, Morgan?"

"I've got something. Hale and I are coming to you."

"Roger that."

A moment later, Hale and Morgan jogged up the dune.

"What is it?" Dec asked.

"Informant in Dakhla got in touch with me," Morgan said. She'd spent a day at the oasis cultivating a few informants. Morgan might have a tough exterior, but when she turned on the charm, people warmed to her instantly. "Anders has been spotted."

Dec cursed. He'd known Anders wouldn't be far away.

Morgan cleared her throat. "And a couple of tourists, young women from Germany, were found murdered in a back alley. They'd been tortured. Multiple cuts and stab wounds."

Dec's jaw tightened. It sounded like Anders' MO. *Fuck.* Dec's hands curled into fists. Two young lives lost, and even though it was Anders who had done the deed, Dec felt the weight of guilt settle over him.

If he'd done the right thing and stopped Anders all those years ago, those girls wouldn't be dead.

The bastard had to be stopped.

Dec stared at the dunes around them. Wondering if Anders was out there, watching them.

"Change up our guard patrols. If Anders is watching us, he'll be trying to learn our routines and find a weak spot. A way in." Dec looked down the hill at Layne again. "We aren't going to give him one."

Chapter Seven

Layne took a long drink of water, stretched her aching shoulders, and glanced over at her tired team. They were sitting around near the tents, drinking, joking.

They'd been so shorthanded in the main part of the dig, she'd ended up hauling buckets of sand to clear a new area. Not only were many of her workers tossing up everything in their bellies, but a few local workers had blamed it on the curse and had left. She sighed and rubbed her forehead. She'd lost count of how many buckets she'd carried, but her achy, tired muscles were the payback. She closed her eyes and dreamed of a nice hot bath.

Yeah, that wasn't happening any time soon.

"Looks like you need this."

Declan's voice made her open her eyes. He was holding out a bottle.

"A Diet Coke!" She snatched it, cracked the lid and took a sweet sip. "The real stuff. Where did you get this?"

"Security secret. Busy day?"

"You could say that." She pulled a face. "Lots of people are sick and I've had workers leave. They say the curse of the mummy is to blame for our bad luck."

"Yeah, I heard."

She rubbed her forehead. She was pretty sure she had dust smeared all over her face. "I'm planning to work on the scroll again this evening."

He reached out and rubbed her cheek. "You're working too hard, Rush."

God, every time he touched her it set her belly jumping. "We're behind."

"Anders was spotted in Dakhla."

The bottom of her stomach dropped away.

Declan's face was grim. "Two young women, tourists, were found dead."

"Oh." Layne pressed a hand to her stomach. She felt sick.

"Get the scroll decoded, Rush, then I suggest we move it and any other valuables to Cairo."

She nodded. "I'm heading to the work tent right now."

In the tent, Layne set her Coke down on the workbench, and carefully pulled the scroll out of her pocket.

God, it was stunning. Looking at it, her shoulders loosened. Staring at this magnificent piece of history filled her with awe and fascination. The troubles of the day faded away.

Her mom and dad would have gotten a huge kick to see it. To see their daughter in charge of finding it and taking care of it. Layne's hands shook and she pressed them to the workbench. She breathed in deep of the warm desert air, the scent nothing like the frigid chill of that long ago snowy day when she'd come home and found them dead.

She glanced over at the gold sarcophagus nearby. She wanted this dig to go well. It was the only way she knew to honor the parents who'd been taken too soon.

She turned back to the scroll. She needed to go over her translations again. She wasn't going to let this beat her. She'd made a mistake somewhere, and she was going to solve it. She set to work, meticulously transcribing her notes down in her notebook.

Layne had no idea how many hours had passed. Outside the work tent, everything was quiet, except for the gentle sound of the desert wind blowing.

Ugh, it was all gibberish. She sat back on her stool and pressed the heels of her hands to her tired eyes. All she had were small fragments talking about birds and the desert. It just didn't make sense.

She sighed and rubbed the back of her neck. It was late. She'd translated as much as she could and now her eyes were crossing. She needed some sleep.

Unable to stop herself, she reached out and stroked the center of the scroll, where there was the empty space and that lone glyph for fierce protector. It was almost like text was missing from here. She touched the strange grooves that Declan had commented on.

The empty space was about the size of her palm. She stared at the little grooves, and then she frowned, tilting her head.

They almost looked like...a dog.

Dog. She froze. The set-animal amulet! She traced the space again. It looked like it was exactly this size.

A flood of excitement made her leap to her feet. She grabbed her radio. "Hey, whoever's on, this is Dr. Rush. I'm heading to grab something out of the safe." She snatched up her flashlight. The set-animal was in the small tent used to hide the safe.

Her flashlight cast a yellow glow on the sand. Beyond the glow, the camp was silent, all the tents dark. As she walked into the extreme desert darkness, her heart clenched. Images of Anders' attack flashed through her head, making her chest tight.

Calm down, Layne. She breathed in a lungful of air. Somewhere out in the darkness, Declan and his team were keeping an eye on things. She let the image of Declan settle in her head and she felt better.

He might annoy her and kiss like a sex god, but he had that dangerous protector vibe going on.

Those kisses...

No. Oh, no. She started across the sand, heading toward the storage tent to get the set-animal artifact. She wasn't going to think of hot lips, and the slick feel of his tongue, and the firm pressure of his fingers biting into her butt.

She stumbled over something and barely kept herself from falling. What the hell? Her flashlight rolled away and she scrambled after it.

When she grabbed it, she aimed the light at what had tripped her.

One of her local workers lay curled in the sand, the end of his jellabiya flapping in the breeze.

Anger surged. She'd had to kick one worker off the dig for drinking. If this man was drunk as well, he was on the first vehicle back to Dakhla, no matter how short they were.

"Hey." She walked closer, shining the light toward his face. "Wake up."

When she nudged him, he rolled onto his back, and all the air in Layne's lungs turned to concrete.

His face was battered beyond recognition and blood soaked the front of his robes.

She screamed, the sound shattering the quiet night. She fell backward and landed on her butt. She couldn't breathe. Her vision blurred, and even after she looked away, all she could see was the poor man's face.

But worse than that, horrible memories of her parents' deaths crowded in.

"Rush!"

A lean shadow raced out of the darkness. She tried to say something, but couldn't do anything more than just shake her head.

Declan took one look at the body and cursed. "Logan, check him out." Then Declan knelt before Layne, blocking her view.

"I'm...sorry." God, her hands were shaking, her voice was shaking. "Just give me a second."

"Breathe."

She nodded, but she felt tears slipping down her

cheeks. She couldn't wipe the images out of her head. "Is he okay?"

"He's dead," Logan said.

Layne felt the color drain from her face. She swayed.

"Screw this." Declan scooped her up.

Layne hadn't been carried by anyone since she was a little girl. But he was so warm, all of that strength radiating off him, and she just buried her face against the side of his neck.

"It's okay, Rush. Hang on."

There was a flap of canvas and he ducked. She realized they were in her personal tent. Her sleeping bag was rolled out neatly, her duffel bag and books off to the side.

He sat and settled her into his lap.

"I'm sorry." She forced herself to dredge up some control. "I don't usually fall apart like this. It just reminded me of my parents."

A big hand stroked her hair. "Take your time. Finding something like this is always a shock." Another soothing stroke.

"God, I feel like a helpless teenager again." But she wasn't. She was a woman who'd forged a life for herself. A career. She wasn't a terrified fifteen year old all alone. "My parents are dead." Her breath hitched again and the old sorrow came roaring in. "They were killed."

Fingers stroked the shell of her ear and for a second she wondered how such a big, tough man could be so comforting.

"It was a home invasion." She shook her head. "I

was fifteen. It was so damned stupid. We were poor and didn't have anything. There was nothing to take, so the attacker took their lives, instead."

"They catch the guy?"

"Yeah. He was a local, high on something and looking to score another fix. He obviously got angry they didn't have anything valuable. I walked in after school and found them." She still remembered the blood soaking the carpet.

"Shit. That's tough, Rush."

"They loved me. I never doubted that." She bit her lip, just letting herself absorb the warmth of him for a second. "He'd beaten them beyond recognition."

Declan's arms tightened around her.

Slowly she felt her strength coming back, the horror receding. "That poor man."

"Don't think of it yet."

"I'm fine now." She reluctantly pulled away from him. In the tight confines of her tent, they were face-to-face. "Thank you."

He touched her hair, pushing it behind her ear. "There you go, Rush."

"I need to know who it was and what happened." Her hands curled. "How did someone get into camp?"

Declan shook his head, his face grim. "No one did. Logan, Hale and I have been patrolling—"

"Someone snuck past you, then—"

"Not possible, Rush."

"All right. Then we need to work out what the hell happened." She rubbed the side of her face.

"Everyone's going to be scared. Theft is one thing..."

"Why don't you stay here?" Declan suggested.

She straightened her shoulders. "Thanks, but no. I'm in charge, and it's my responsibility to take care of my people."

She thought she saw a spark of admiration in Declan's gray eyes.

"Come on then." He helped her up.

They walked over to where she'd found the man, and she saw Logan had covered the body with a sheet. A few of the local security guards milled around nearby.

Logan's big silhouette appeared out of the shadows. He was holding a handgun. Hale and Morgan appeared behind him.

"Worker came into camp like this. I tracked his footprints out into the dunes. Looks like he met someone out there."

Declan nodded. "So we probably saw him walking around, knew he was one of ours, and didn't question it."

"You're saying he was in on this?" Layne wrapped her arms around herself. The desert breeze felt downright chilly now.

"Looks like he was poking around the work tent," Logan said.

She closed her eyes. "So he probably saw the scroll."

"And he met someone," Logan growled. "And that someone beat the shit out of him."

"He wandered back in here, maybe looking for

help, but didn't make it." Declan scanned the shadow-soaked dunes. "What a fucking mess."

"Is it Anders?" she asked.

"I don't know." Declan's tone was hard. "But I'm going to damn well find out. Right now, though, I need to call the authorities and deal with finding the dead man's family."

She nodded. "And I need to wake everyone up and tell them what's happened."

Her long night was about to get longer.

***

In the early hours of the morning, Dec faced his team. "Report?"

"We scoured the dunes," Logan said with a frown. "Nothing."

Dammit. "Anders is out there. I contacted Darcy. She's looking into the dead worker. Name's Karim Abasi. If he's received any payments from anyone, she'll find it. Police out of Dakhla are on the way. They'll take the man's body."

"So it was probably this Karim who sabotaged the scaffold," Hale said.

Dec shrugged a shoulder. "Probably. We have to assume he's been feeding Anders information as well. And Anders knows about the scroll."

Dec looked over to where Layne was talking to her people. Everyone was shocked and horrified. The local workers were huddled together, whispering. Rush looked exhausted.

"All right, Morgan and Hale, you're on shift.

Make sure no one gets in. You see anyone moving around, anything suspicious, call me."

"You got it, boss," Hale said.

Morgan nodded.

"Logan, grab some shut eye."

His friend tossed him a lazy salute.

Dec headed toward Layne. He grabbed her shoulders. "Okay, Rush. Bed."

Her eyes widened.

"Not with me." Images tried to crowd into his head, but he regretfully shut them down. "In your tent. You're asleep on your feet." He herded her toward her tent.

"I still need to grab the set-animal artifact. That's where I was headed when..." she swallowed. Then she grabbed Dec's wrists. "Declan, before I found Karim, I realized what the fierce protector hieroglyph and those small grooves on the scroll mean. The set-animal amulet...I think it fits into the scroll. I think it's the key to decoding the scroll and whatever is written on it."

All the tiredness had washed off her face. Like it did every time she talked about her work.

"Okay, Rush. That's pretty interesting, but you need some sleep."

She frowned. "Are you my mother now?"

"Hell, no. But you need sleep before you fall down. You can test your theory tomorrow."

She cast one longing glance at her work tent.

Dec's gut clenched. Hell, that look on her face, the longing. It got to him. Made him wonder what he needed to do to make her look at him like that.

Damn. He was getting hard.

"Oh, I left the scroll on my workbench—"

"I'll lock it away myself."

They walked down to the personal tents. Everyone was heading back to their sleeping bags. Outside of her tent, she hesitated.

"What is it?" he asked.

She sank her teeth into her bottom lip. "I'm not sure I can sleep. Finding Karim like that..."

And the memories of her parents. Hell, he'd seen the file on her, knew her parents were deceased. But it hadn't mentioned that she'd found their bodies, or carved a career and a life for herself, all on her own.

He touched her hair. "The adrenaline will fade soon, and you'll crash. You'll find you can't stay awake."

She tilted her head. "Speaking from experience?"

"Yeah." He reached out and stroked her jaw.

Her eyelids fluttered. "I used to have nightmares, after my parents. That their killer would come for me."

Her soft voice made him want to sweep her into his arms. "I'll watch over your tent, Rush. Nothing's going to happen to you."

With that reassurance, she unzipped her tent. "Declan, thank you."

"You're welcome." He pushed her inside. "Now rest."

Chapter Eight

Layne headed over to the kitchen tent for a coffee. She'd slept surprisingly well, but she guessed she had Declan to thank for that. Just knowing he was outside, watching over her like...well, not a guardian angel. Declan Ward didn't inspire images of halos and wings, more like a fallen angel. He had a face perfectly suited for that, a fallen angel ready to sweep a girl into sin.

She shook her head. Okay, maybe she didn't get as much sleep as she'd thought. And the dull headache was a reminder of what had happened the night before.

"Hey, Doc, are you all right?" Piper appeared, concern stamped all over her face.

"I'm fine. Declan and his security team did their job very well."

"I can't believe you found Karim like that."

Layne stepped around Piper and entered the tent. She poured herself a black coffee and studiously tried to *not* think about that moment when she'd found Karim.

"It's Karim and his family who need the sympathy." She noted that there was still a lot of breakfast food on the table. She frowned. Usually everyone devoured it in minutes.

When she turned back, Piper was rubbing the back of her neck and looked uncomfortable.

Layne's heart sank. "Spit it out." She took a bracing sip of coffee.

"When everyone heard what happened, that Karim was dead, well, everyone blamed the curse. Saying the spirit of the mummy rose up to take revenge for disturbing his eternal rest."

Layne released a long breath and pressed a finger to her throbbing temple. "Well, the guy who beat Karim to death sure wasn't a spirit."

Piper winced.

Instantly, Layne felt bad. "Sorry. Sorry, you didn't deserve that. I'm just frustrated and tired. If I hadn't known Declan was watching my tent, I probably wouldn't have gotten any sleep."

"Oh." Piper's eyebrows rose. "So, the sexy security man provided a personal security service." Now those eyebrows waggled.

Layne took a hasty sip of her coffee. "Why did I ask you to join this dig again?"

"Because I'm brilliant, am one of the few assistants who'll put up with your workaholic ways, and you like me."

Layne made a harrumphing sound. "I'm sure you're mistaken."

"Oh, and I do all the boring, dirty jobs so you don't have to."

"Ah, that was it." Layne drank more coffee.

Piper touched her arm. "I really am glad you're okay."

Layne smiled. "Thanks, Piper." She glanced out towards the main excavation. It seemed eerily quiet. "Is everyone down in the dig?"

"Weeeellll—"

Layne groaned. "What now?"

"It's what I was trying to tell you. It's the curse. Most of the workers have left and returned to Dakhla. They refuse to work if there is a—"

"Curse. Got it." She absorbed the impact and looked over at the work tent. Right now, she needed to work. "I'm heading back to work on the sarcophagus. You and Dr. Stiller work out the most important work to do next, and set whatever workers we have left doing that. Can you handle things down there?"

"You got it, Doc."

"Thanks, Piper." Layne headed across the sand. The sun was already getting hot. Today was going to be a scorcher.

Someone fell into step beside her.

"Morning, Rush," Declan said. "You look like hell."

"Gee, thanks. Way to make my morning better."

"Get any sleep?"

"A few hours, thanks to you."

"I spoke with the authorities this morning." He shrugged his broad shoulders. "Nothing they can do. Suspect it was a thief who killed Karim."

"At least they aren't blaming the curse."

"Yeah. Sorry to hear about your workers."

She set her shoulders back. "We'll find more. For now, I have work to do. I need that set-animal amulet. I want to see if it fits—"

When he pulled it out of his pocket, she smiled at him.

"Figured you'd be keen to test your theory," he said. "I also had Hale put the scroll in the work tent."

He followed her into the tent, and the moment she laid eyes on the scroll, she forgot about her crappy morning.

She put the amulet down and snapped on gloves. She gently rolled out the scroll and then picked up the set-animal. Holding it over the scroll, she hesitated, her gaze meeting Declan's.

He nodded.

She set it down and it clicked into place.

"It fits!" She grinned, then leaned over the scroll, murmuring to herself. "Declan, the glyphs on the set-animal tie in with the ones on the scroll. It makes sense now!"

"The missing piece of the puzzle," he said.

She pulled her notepad open, grabbed her pen, and sat on her stool. She set to work and Declan leaned over her shoulder, watching.

It scattered her thoughts a little. She could feel the heat coming off him. He was just too masculine.

She took a breath and started decoding the ancient symbols.

One stumped her. Dammit. She scribbled some ideas, scratched them out.

"It's the symbol for west," Declan said. "It's a

very old variant, but I'm pretty sure it's west."

She stilled, and slowly wrote *west* in her notes. "In the desert to the west. That works."

"And this other one you're having trouble with. I think it means small or tiny."

"God, you're right." She scribbled furiously, then she tilted her head back and looked at his rugged face. "We're not a bad team."

She watched his face shutter and it made her chest tighten.

"So, what's the final translation?" he asked.

Right. Translation. She cleared her throat. "To find your way to the desert in the west, to the House of Seth's beloved."

Declan frowned. "Got any more?"

"Yes. It joins up with what I translated yesterday." She ran her finger along the text. "*True believer, do not be taken in by the lies of the falcon. Use the scroll, hidden with Itennu, loyal servant of the true god of gold. Solve the riddles of the true god, to find your way to the desert in the west, to the House of Seth's beloved, then the place of the small birds, where he is king.*" She took a breath. "*To the oasis of Zerzura.*" Her hands trembled. "It's a map to Zerzura."

"This is what Anders is after," Declan said grimly.

"It can't be real, Declan. This must be a spiritual journey. Like the path to the afterlife, the dead have to pass through various gates and solve riddles. The desert in the west symbolizes the afterlife, where the dying sun sets each day."

"This sounds pretty real to me, Rush."

God, she hoped not. But at the same time... "Keep your voice down. We can't have anyone overhearing, regardless." If word got out, they'd be inundated with treasure hunters, looters, thieves, adventurers, rival archeologists. She pressed a palm to her forehead. "Zerzura is a legend. Lost cities can't stay lost in this day and age of satellite images."

"It doesn't matter. Anders thinks that map is real."

And he wouldn't hesitate to kill for it. "What should we do?"

"We need to get the scroll out of here and you need to close down the dig."

"What?" She shot to her feet. "I can't shut the dig—"

"Layne, you don't have enough workers anyway," he said quietly. "Which I'm guessing Anders has something to do with."

"What?"

"I'm guessing he poisoned the food, with Karim's help."

She rubbed her head. "Dammit." She'd wanted this dig to be a huge success. Now it was just a disaster, and a man was dead.

She couldn't risk any more lives.

With a heavy heart, she nodded. "Fine. I'll let everyone finish out the day, then I'll close the dig. But only temporarily. Until you find Anders."

"Tomorrow, we'll head to Luxor and take the jet back to Cairo." Declan grabbed her shoulder, and gave it a light squeeze. "It's only temporary."

So why did she still feel like a failure?

***

Layne stared at her dig team.

It was a pitifully small group.

They only had a few workers left, and they'd barely gotten much done today. Everyone was dragging, after having spent the day doing twice as many jobs just to get anything accomplished.

She scraped a hand through her hair. Behind the group, Declan and his team stood, quiet and still.

"Okay, Aaron, send the local workers back to the oasis. They have a week off."

The archeologist spluttered. "What? You're going to send the only people we have—?"

"We don't have enough workers, I know it and you know it." She put her hands on her hips. "I want you to head into the oasis and recruit more workers." She did some quick math in her head. "Up the hourly rate."

He frowned. "That'll cut into the dig budget—"

"I am in charge of the budget. You let me worry about that." Without workers, there'd be no dig to spend the money on.

Aaron scowled. "We hired all the best workers from Dakhla. There won't be more."

"Fine. Take a jeep and go to Luxor."

He gave her a stiff nod.

Layne eyed Piper and the others. "You guys

have seven days off. Head into Dakhla, or Luxor, or Cairo if you prefer. Relax. Refresh."

The grad students all grinned and fist-bumped. Piper gave a slow nod.

By the time the sun was setting, the dig was a ghost town. Layne finished making herself a sandwich and headed over to the fire.

Declan sat in the sand, Logan and Hale with him.

She sat. "Where's Morgan?"

"She's on watch with the guards," Declan answered.

Layne had no trouble imagining the woman prowling around in the darkness. As Layne ate, the men talked, ribbing each other, telling jokes. She enjoyed the banter. She'd never had siblings, and in the foster home where she'd stayed, no one teased or joked good-naturedly. Besides, she'd been focused on studying and getting good grades. She'd wanted to make a good life for herself and make her parents proud.

Staring out at the silent dig, she wondered if they'd be proud of this screw up.

She stood. "I'll be in the work tent for a bit before I head to bed." She murmured her goodnights and trudged across the sand.

She lost herself in the scroll again. It helped dull the pain of knowing her dig was at best delayed and at worst falling apart. She double-checked her translation, making meticulous notes.

"I'm sorry."

She jerked. "Goddammit, Declan, make some

damn noise."

He grunted and leaned on the table beside her. All masculine heat, radiating that intensity that seemed to reach inside her and make her tingle.

"What are you sorry about?" she grumped. "Scaring the hell out of me?"

"No. That the dig isn't working out the way you wanted."

"Not your fault." She set her pen down. "You've actually been the most helpful person here." And wasn't that just strange.

He gave her a small smile. "My mother likes to tell me that out of the darkest moments, the best answers often emerge."

"That's kind of deep for a treasure hunter." She wondered when Declan would have needed his mother to tell him that.

"She likes to get spiritual on me sometimes."

"Do you believe her?"

"Not really. The darkest moments just seem dark and shitty and drag on far longer than you want them to."

Her heart clenched. "Declan...what happened? With Anders?"

He was quiet for so long, she thought he was going to ignore her.

"My SEAL team was on a joint mission with his team in the Middle East. I discovered Anders was keeping a little dungeon. He was holding locals there. Torturing them."

Her stomach turned over. "How could anyone do that?"

"He's a psychopath, Layne. He likes to kill, and he feels no remorse. He had men, women, children..." Declan shook his head.

"You stopped him? You saved those people?"

When she watched Declan's jaw go tight, she knew that wasn't what had happened.

"I was ordered to leave them there to suffer, until we had enough evidence against Anders."

A tense silence fell.

Layne shook her head. "You aren't built like that."

A muscle ticked in his jaw. "I disobeyed orders. Took my team in."

"You saved them."

"No. Most of them were already dead. I think Anders knew I was on to him."

Her chest tightened. And it still haunted Declan to this day. "You did the right thing."

"Anders got off. Not enough evidence. Because I disobeyed orders, the bastard avoided jail." Declan shook his head. "Sorry. Didn't mean to get into all this. Look, Rush, I know things aren't working out how you wanted, but I know you can pull through this. Hell, your dedication and enthusiasm alone—I've never seen someone so packed with those two qualities."

Warmth spread through her chest. "Thank you."

"So, what's left with the scroll?"

"Nothing. I've translated it all." She tore out the sheet with her notes. "It's all right here." She tucked it into her pocket. "For anyone crazy enough to follow it out to the middle of nowhere, in one of the most unforgiving deserts in the world."

"You should get some sleep. We'll make an early start in the morning to Luxor. I'll put the scroll back in the safe."

She nodded. "Good night, Declan."

"Night, Rush."

When Layne got to her tent, she realized just how tired she was. She managed to get her boots off and then fell, fully clothed into her sleeping bag.

Sleep took her and the dreams took over. A jumble of crazy images she couldn't pull apart.

When someone slammed a hand over her mouth, she thought it was part of the dream.

But then she came awake with a jerk, her scream muffled against a large hand. She was jerked backward against a hard, male body.

Panic fired, her pulse spiking. She wasn't letting whoever this was kill her or get their hands on the scroll.

Layne started struggling and slammed her head back, the back of her head colliding with her attacker's face.

Chapter Nine

Dec muttered a curse. "Shit, Rush, it's me." He kept his voice a whisper. "Now be quiet."

The struggling woman in his arms stilled. When he judged she was calm enough, he uncovered her mouth.

Her head whipped around. "Dammit, Declan." She was pissed, but keeping her voice down. "What the hell are you doing?"

"There's a team infiltrating the camp right now. We spotted them coming."

She gasped. "Anders."

"Yeah, and I'm guessing he's got some not very friendly people with him. We're outnumbered."

Dismay covered her face. "They're coming for the sarcophagus and the scroll."

"Yeah."

She swore under her breath. "We need to get to the safe and get the scroll and the set-animal amulet. And Aaron's still here. He didn't leave for Luxor—"

Gunshots echoed in the night.

Declan cursed. "No time. We have to go. Now!" He pulled her toward the entrance. "Boots. And grab your emergency pack."

Even though he could sense her fear, she followed his orders. She got her boots on and slipped her pack onto her back.

Dec already had his, and he pulled out his SIG Sauer.

Layne eyed the handgun. She took a deep breath and followed him out.

Outside, he saw flashlights arcing through the dig. Two vehicles stood, lights on, illuminating the main excavation site. He saw shadows moving at the storage tents.

He grabbed her arm and pulled her away from the action and into the shadows. There was a brisk wind blowing.

Dec touched his ear. "Everyone okay?"

His team checked in.

"All clear," Morgan said.

"Idiot stepped on Hale," Logan said. "But we're fine."

"Okay. Where are you?"

"Eastern side. Five hundred meters out of camp and watching the show."

Shit. He and Rush were on the other side of the camp.

"Roger that. Anyone see Stiller? He was in his tent."

"That's a negative," Logan said.

Not good. "Okay. Get to safety. The doc and I are on the western side. Let's lay low, and then rendezvous at the prearranged emergency point."

The wind blew harder, spitting sand in their faces. At least it would muffle noise, and hopefully help conceal their footprints.

"We need to get out of camp and meet up with my team."

Rush nodded. "I hate leaving these bastards with free range of my dig—"

"Yeah, sorry I misplaced my army, otherwise I'd take them down."

A hint of white teeth in the dark. "And there go all those superhero delusions I had about you."

"Come on, Rush. Even while I'm rescuing you you're busting my balls." He tugged her down a dune and deeper into the desert.

They hadn't gone far when he heard voices raised in excitement. Dec turned. The headlights of one car perfectly illuminated Aaron Stiller's skinny form. He was pushed hard by the thug holding his arm and the archeologist fell to his knees.

"No," Layne said, pressing a hand to her mouth.

Then a tall, broad figure appeared.

Everything in Dec's body went still. Ian Anders.

He had a clean-cut face for such an evil person. He was wearing all black and staring at Stiller with calculation. Then he held out his hands.

Dec heard Layne gasp. Anders was holding the scroll and the set-animal amulet.

"Can Stiller translate the scroll?" Dec asked.

She nodded. "Without a doubt."

"Shit." There was nothing they could do. Dec chewed it over and realized he needed help. He pulled out his satellite phone and thumbed in Darcy's number.

His sister, reliable as always, answered on the

first ring. "Declan?"

"Darcy, I don't have long. Anders has raided the camp. He has the scroll and one of the archeologists. Rush says the guy can decode the scroll."

"The map to Zerzura," his sister said grimly.

"Yes. I need you to call in Callum. Tell him to come in with help."

"I'm on it. What else—"

The scream of static filled his ear and his phone went dead. With a curse, he turned it off. Next, he touched his earpiece. "Logan? You there?"

Nothing.

He yanked his earpiece from his ear. "Dammit to hell."

"What?"

In the starlight, he could make out Layne's pale face. "They're jamming our comms."

There were more loud voices from the direction of the camp. Dec glanced over his shoulder...and saw flashlights heading in their direction.

"Dammit. Run, Rush."

They sprinted through the sand. Layne tripped, but Dec grabbed her arm. She righted herself and kept running.

The wind grew stronger and Dec felt the whip of sand against his skin. He scanned ahead. The vague outlines of the dunes were all he could see. There were no good hiding places.

Suddenly, a large shape loomed over them. Dec's pulse spiked and he brought his gun up.

"Dec."

Dec lowered his weapon. "Shit, Logan. I almost blew your head off."

Logan snorted. "Come on."

Dec grabbed Layne's arm and soon they reached the bottom of the dune. "Logan, plan?"

"Bury ourselves in the sand."

"Hey, boss man."

Dec heard Morgan's voice but didn't see her.

"Down here."

Dec just made out the two bulges in the sand that he guessed were Morgan and Hale. He nodded. "Let's do it. Rush, lie down."

She did, pressing her belly to the sand. Dec quickly covered her with sand.

"Stay still and quiet."

She nodded but he knew she had to be scared. He touched her head, then quickly set to work burying himself right beside her.

The voices got louder.

Under the thin layer of sand, Dec stayed very still. He'd had practice at sitting quietly, waiting, on missions. Patience was a hell of a valuable skill, along with calm under fire.

Someone was shouting in Arabic.

From just meters away.

He kept his breathing calm and waited. He felt something shift right by his hand...then slim fingers slid into his under the sand. *Layne.* He gently tangled his fingers with hers and held on.

Dec willed these guys to move on. To go somewhere else. If these goons shined their lights down, they might notice Dec's and the team's hiding place.

After what felt like an eternity, the voices drifted away.

Soon, all Dec could hear was the whistle of the wind.

Finally, he sat up and shook the sand out of his hair. He heard the others doing the same. He helped Layne up.

"Nice work, Rush."

"I thought I was going to faint. They were practically on top of us."

"Come on." He saw the glow of flashlights not far away. "They're still looking for us and something tells me they'll be back." He hauled her to her feet. "Time to go."

Together, they all set off, trudging through the sand.

"I managed to get a call into Darcy before they jammed us," Declan said to the others. "I called in Cal."

"Good," Logan said.

"For now, we make our way to Dakhla—"

"Boss?"

He frowned. "Yes, Morgan?"

"I think we have a problem." Morgan was pointing ahead of them.

Dec looked up and drew in a sharp breath. "Oh, shit."

"What?" Layne's voice was shaky.

"Look ahead."

"I see sand dunes."

"Above them."

"I see the black night sky." There was confusion in her voice.

"No stars."

She stared ahead, then gasped. "Something's blocking out the stars."

As she said it, the wind picked up even more, howling at them.

Dec's mind raced as he tried to find an escape plan to keep them alive. Behind them, was a team of very organized and well-funded antiquities thieves.

And in front of them, brewing like a boiling witch's broth, was a wild desert sandstorm.

"Come on. We go on a bit farther, then we'll take cover." If they burrowed in too early, the thieves might catch them.

"If we wait too long, the sandstorm could kill us," Layne shouted. "I've been through one out here on another dig. And I've heard some pretty bad stories."

"Then we'd better get the timing right. Everyone, open your emergency packs."

Everyone pulled scarves and goggles out of the backpacks and slipped them on.

They pushed on until the edge of the sandstorm swallowed them. Soon the lights behind them disappeared. Hell, everything disappeared.

The sand was pinging off his skin hard and stinging. He tapped Logan's arm. The man would know what to do.

Dec grabbed Layne's arm. There was no way she'd hear him over the howl of the wind. He pulled her down in the sand and yanked his backpack off. He pulled out the small, plain canvas tent he had in his pack.

It wasn't fancy. You didn't want mesh in a desert to let all the dust and sand in. He quickly set it up. It was a solo tent—sleek and streamlined. It was going to be a tight fit for two of them.

He urged her in. He tried to spot the rest of his team, but the storm was too bad. The wind was tearing at him now like a wild beast. Logan and the others were all trained and experienced. He knew he didn't need to worry about them.

Dec followed Layne into the tent. It only took a second to seal the tent behind them.

He turned to face her. There was only just enough room to sit up and his head brushed the top. He pressed a button on his watch and the face glowed. It gave just enough light to make her out. She looked kind of cute with the huge goggles dominating her face.

The wind was making the canvas flap, and its wail was like a mob of monsters right on top of them.

He saw Layne's hands were clenched tightly together.

Dec pulled her into his arms and held on. She buried her face against his chest and wrapped her arms around him.

Funny how in that instant, Dec wouldn't trade being stuck in the middle of a deadly sandstorm for anything.

***

Callum Ward gunned his motorbike and leaned into the curve.

Evening was falling in Denver and the city lights twinkled above him. His sweet little Ducati wanted to go faster—she'd clearly missed him while he'd been trekking through the Amazon. But as he whizzed through the LoDo area, he stuck to the speed limit. Mostly. He promised himself he'd take her out of the city one day and let her knock his teeth into the back of his head.

His jaw tightened. *After* he'd rescued his brother.

Cal pulled up in front of the Treasure Hunter Security warehouse. Lights were still on inside and he knew Darcy would be busy with her computers.

He pulled his helmet off and headed inside.

Darcy looked up and as soon as she saw him, rushed over. "Thank God you're here." She threw her arms around him. "I didn't think you'd be back until tomorrow."

"One idiot anthropologist safely retrieved." He pulled back and frowned at her worried face. "D, what's going on? On our last call you said you were worried about Dec and his job…"

She pressed her hands together. "The dig got raided three hours ago. I've lost contact with Dec and the team."

Cal cursed. He strode toward the computers. The thoughts of taking a few days off to ride his bike and go rock climbing in the mountains evaporated. "What do we know?"

"Anders raided the dig with Silk Road thugs. Dec and Layne, the lead archeologist, got separated from Logan and the others. I have no idea if they managed to meet up." Darcy scraped a hand through her hair, messing it up. A surefire sign she was agitated. "Something jammed our signal. Plus I just checked—" her blue-gray eyes were drowning in worry "—and a huge desert sandstorm hit their location a few hours ago. I can't even pick up the emergency trackers in any of the team's watches."

Fuck. Cal sucked in a deep breath. "Any good news?"

"No. Dec said Anders captured one of the other archeologists and a scroll that leads to Zerzura."

"Look, they'll be fine. Dec is good at this work, D. He'll get himself, the team, and the archeologists out of there."

"Cal, it's *Anders.*"

Hell. Cal's gut went hard. She was right. That meant his brother was unlikely to back off and Anders was a dangerous psychopath.

"I'm going in," Cal said. "Where's Coop?"

"Ronin's on a job in Canada."

"Damn." Cal rubbed his forehead, running through logistics in his head. He had to get to Egypt...fast. "I know who to call. Get me flights to Cairo. When we land, I'll call." He pulled his sister in for a hard hug. "Keep trying to contact Dec."

She nodded. "Cal, I have a bad feeling. I'm scared for Dec."

"He's tougher than titanium." Cal cupped her

cheek. "I'll find him."

She released a slow breath and managed a nod.

Cal strode out to his bike, tugging his helmet on. It was only then that he let his worry show.

***

Layne woke up warm and snug.

She blinked, focusing on the hard arm wrapped around her waist. She shifted and realized she was clutched tightly in Declan's arms, her back nestled to his hard chest, her butt snuggled to his hard—

He was stroking her arm slowly, seemingly relaxed.

Then it all crashed in on her. The sandstorm. The raid.

She shot upright, bumping the top of the tent and dislodging a rain of dust. She started coughing and felt her goggles resting around her neck.

She felt Declan move.

"Either we survived, or the afterlife is dusty as hell." She turned toward him. "It's morning, and it feels like the sun is getting pretty warm. I can't believe we fell asleep!"

"I wasn't asleep."

She eyed him. The dark stubble on his cheeks just made him look sexier and more dangerous. But he was alert. She realized he'd been watching over her during the sandstorm, protecting her as always.

She didn't let herself think, she just leaned down and kissed him.

His arms clamped around her and yanked her down on his chest. Layne cupped his rough cheeks and poured everything into the kiss. He groaned, then bit her bottom lip, making her moan. His hands slid down her sides.

"When we're safe, I'm planning to strip your clothes off and fuck you," he growled. "Every way I know how."

She pulled back, staring into his glittering gray eyes. She licked her lips, savoring the taste of him. "Oh? What happened to your 'I'm too dark and brooding for you' speech?"

He sank a hand into her hair and tugged her head back. "You are such a pain in my ass."

"Good. You need it. So you've decided I'm not too sweet and innocent for you?"

His thumb traced her lips, the air charging even more. She nipped at the hard pad of his thumb and something molten flared in his eyes.

"I never said you were sweet."

She nipped again. "Good. Because, Declan Ward, I can be very not-sweet when I want to be."

He groaned again. "I'm going to make you pay for giving me a damn painful hard-on. Especially when we need to get moving and there is nothing I can do about it."

Reluctantly, she pulled away and sat on the layer of sand that had infiltrated their tent. She patted his chest. "Poor thing."

He sat up. "Careful, payback is a bitch."

Layne grinned cheekily at him. Considering thieves had raided her dig and she'd just survived a sandstorm, she was feeling pretty good.

They packed up their meager belongings and climbed out of the tent.

The morning sun was rising in the sky and the temperature was getting warm. She turned around, taking in the view, her stomach dropping.

"What the hell?" she murmured.

Beside her, Declan cursed.

Everything looked...completely different.

They were still in the desert, but the rolling dunes of golden sand were gone. Ahead was a white salt flat. There were some strange rock formations in the distance. Everything was shades of bleached brown.

There was no sign of the dig.

"Nothing looks familiar." Layne swallowed.

"Shit. Powerful sandstorms can move vast quantities of sand around." He scanned the area around them. "I don't see Logan and the others."

He cupped his hands and called out.

No response.

"Rush, can you pack up the tent? I'll take a look for the others. They can't be far away."

By the time Layne wrestled the tent into a neat pile, Declan came back, his face the grimmest she'd ever seen it.

"No sign of them. And my satellite phone is completely dead."

"How can they not be here?"

"I don't know. But they're trained soldiers, they can take care of themselves. I can't worry about them right now. We need to work out our plan." He studied the rugged watch on his wrist and she peered at it. He tilted it in her direction. "It has a built-in GPS tracker. I think our best bet is to still head northeast. Toward Dakhla."

She spun. "It's miles away! It'll take all day to walk there."

"Yes, but it's a large landmark we can't miss. There's food, water, and shelter at the end." He held up his backpack. "We only have a small amount of water with us."

Layne chewed on her lip, and for a second let herself worry about her dig, the artifacts, Aaron, Zerzura. Damn Ian Anders for all of this. And now because of this crazy asshole, she and Declan were lost in the desert.

"What about Zerzura?" she asked quietly. The thought of Anders desecrating the place made her sick.

Declan ran his fingers down her cheek. "Your safety comes first."

Warmth trickled through her. "Okay. Dakhla it is."

"Worst case, my brother's coming. He can track me from this." Declan shook his wrist.

But as they headed off, Layne knew that Callum Ward was days away from reaching them.

The ground was rocky and sandy, but at least the flatter ground was easier than traversing the large dunes. As they walked, the sun grew hotter, beating down on them. Layne wished for her hat, but made do with her scarf, wrapping it around her head.

Declan warned her to take tiny sips of her water and make it last. She did, but the small mouthfuls hardly quenched her rabid thirst.

Just keep walking, Rush.

Declan, damn him, looked like he was out for a stroll. He walked with a loose-limbed, easy stride she envied, while she felt like she was dragging each foot through the sand.

"I'll buy you a cold beer when we get to Dakhla, Rush."

"Make it a Diet Coke, and you're on," she said.

"You don't drink?"

She shook her head. "Guy who killed my parents was high as a kite, unaware that he destroyed my entire life. I've never touched drugs or alcohol."

Declan nodded. "Diet Coke it is." He paused for a moment. "Bet your parents would be proud as hell of the life you've made for yourself."

She smiled. "Yeah. I think so. They were the ones who sent me down this path. Trips to the museum. Documentaries."

"Meanwhile, my parents tried to get me interested...by dragging me around dusty old digs, and sitting me in the corner of dad's office." A faint smile. "It had the opposite effect."

"Ah, I hate to break it to you, Ward, but you work on digs and in museums now."

"Yeah. I guess I always liked it, but once I hit my teens I knew I wanted to join the military. I think protecting artifacts is important, but protecting people, fighting for my country, that just spoke to something in me."

"Sounds like you did a good job of it."

His face changed, turning hard as stone. "Sometimes."

"You can't blame yourself for the people Anders killed. That's on him, not you."

A muscle ticked in Declan's jaw. "I don't want to talk about it."

"You can't bury the past, Declan. It just pops up to haunt you, otherwise."

"Not open for discussion."

Here was a good man, haunted by his past. So much he couldn't even acknowledge all the good he did. "If you ignore it, then it just terrorizes you in your sleep, dogs your steps in the daylight, and blindsides you when you least expect it."

He stopped and spun, his face tight. "So, do you think of finding your murdered parents all the time?"

She absorbed the blow, and tucked her hair back under her scarf.

"Shit. Sorry." He heaved out a breath and looked away. "That was out of line."

She stared at his tense back. "I think about them. But I've learned to remember the good stuff first. I bet you have loads of good memories from your time as a SEAL. Do you ever think of those?"

He shoved his hands in his pockets. "The past is the past."

"The past is a lesson to absorb and learn from. Whatever our personal experiences, we have to face them and learn to live with them. I had a lot of therapy and now, I'm focused on building my career."

"Because of what happened?"

"Yes. It still affects me. I have no family. It's easy to feel pretty darn alone in this world." Dammit, she hadn't meant to say that. "What happened with Anders, it's eating you alive, Declan."

Silence fell. It was just the two of them and the desert. She waited a few more beats. He wasn't going to talk. She sighed.

"It was my fault." Declan didn't look at her. "I didn't save those people, and because of my screw up, he got off."

The words were hard as rock, and he spat them out as fast as bullets.

"You did what you thought was right," she said quietly.

A vicious shake of his head. "Knowing they died, knowing he's gone on killing. That's all on me, Rush. That's not something you face and make peace with."

Yes, she could see—for a man who lived to protect people, the deaths of those people had carved out a piece of his soul. "You were between a rock and a hard place. Go in early, save lives, but forgo the evidence. Let the people die, but get the evidence. There was no win-win situation, Declan."

"Instead, I waited just long enough for almost all those people to die and Anders still walked free."

She could feel the tension radiating off him. "I'm sure the few who survived were grateful." She touched his arm. "I'm so sorry, Declan."

"Bastard is still out there terrorizing people." Declan touched her healing cheek.

"You did your best. God, you aren't a superhero, expected to be perfect and win the day every time. Cut yourself some slack."

They stared at each other for a long moment. When Declan smiled, she felt like she'd won a prize.

"Your sweetness is showing, Rush."

She snorted. "And your badassness is still firmly in place." Her gaze shifted past him and she blinked. "I see people ahead. Look."

He spun. "It's a heat mirage. No telling what those shapes are."

He was right, the shimmer made it hard to tell what the hazy, dark, shifting shapes were, but they sure looked like people to her. "Let's check it out."

They pushed on. The mirage felt like it wasn't getting any closer. But those tantalizing shapes made her hope for safety, water, and rest.

"I want a huge glass of cold water. No, a bucket of it. I'll drink until I pop, then tip it over my head." She groaned. "Oh, a cold bath has never sounded so good."

Declan grunted.

She elbowed him in the side. "Come on, what do you want once we reach Dakhla?"

"You."

She stumbled to a stop.

His gaze traced her face. "A cold shower first would be good, then you spread out on a bed, naked. All mine."

All the air in her lungs rushed out. The heat filtering through her now had nothing to do with the sun. "Don't get me more hot and bothered!"

He grinned and some of that darkness that had been plaguing him eased from his face. "Is that what I'm doing?"

"Shush. No more about being naked."

Now he groaned.

Soon, the shapes in the distance stopped moving.

Layne's heart sank.

They weren't people or trees. They were rocks.

The strange rock formations rose up. Some were like large balls at the top, narrowing down at the base. Others were straight, like pillars spearing upward.

Layne swallowed, trying to dampen her dry throat. "I've never heard of anything like this close to Dakhla."

"Me neither," Declan said. "But we can't be far away. Keep moving, Rush."

They did. They stopped a few times to rest and eat the nutrition bars from their backpacks. Layne was horribly aware that their water bottles were almost empty.

It felt like they'd been walking for days.

Her face felt pink from sunburn, her lips were chapped, and she was so tired and thirsty.

She kept walking, barely noticing that she was dragging her feet now, her legs feeling like blocks of lead.

One foot in front of the other.

Keep walking.

One.

Two.

Three.

Layne fell to her knees.

She blinked, trying to focus, trying to get her legs working. But all she could do was stay there on her knees, her hands dragging in the sand.

Chapter Ten

Dec suddenly realized that Layne wasn't with him anymore.

He turned and spotted her a few feet back, on her knees, wavering. He rushed back and skidded to his knees beside her. "Shit, sweetheart."

She licked her cracked lips. "Sorry. Need a rest."

She needed more than that. He was pretty sure heat exhaustion was setting in. He cupped her face, checking her eyes.

"Here." He pulled his water bottle out.

"No." She pushed it away. "You need it—"

"I need you alive."

"You could go on. Bring help back."

His entire body rebelled at the thought. No fucking way was he leaving her here alone. "Hell, no. We are doing this together, Rush."

She'd been such a damn trooper he hadn't realized how badly she was doing. He slid an arm around her and hefted her up. He took as much of her weight as he could and they kept moving.

What he didn't tell her, what he was most worried about, was that by his calculations, they should have reached the Dakhla Oasis about an hour ago.

She stumbled, pushing into his side. "I'm glad you're with me, Declan."

"Me too." He hugged her tighter.

"Wish this sand was near a beach." She had a goofy smile on her face. "A nice cold beach. With cold, frothy drinks and palm trees."

"When we get out of here, Rush, I'm taking you to the beach. I'd like to see you in a bikini."

"I have a teeny, tiny red one."

"Tease."

He felt her slow down more. "Declan…my feet are really hurting. I've been ignoring them, but I can't anymore."

He forced her to sit and carefully pulled off her boots and socks. She made small pained sounds that arrowed into him.

When he saw her feet, he cursed. "Layne."

Sand had gotten in and had rubbed her feet raw in patches. It had to hurt like hell, and she hadn't said a thing.

She managed a tired smile. "Sore feet, sunburn, tangled hair, and chapped lips. I must look like hell."

He cupped her cheek and forced her to look at him. "You're beautiful. Smart, committed, enthusiastic. The most beautiful woman I've known."

Her lips tipped up. "I think you've had too much sun."

Dec pulled out his tiny first aid kit. He didn't have much, but he had some small bandages. He set to work covering the worst of the raw marks.

He emptied her socks and boots of sand and slipped them back on. When he tightened the laces, she winced, but set her shoulders back.

"I'm ready," she said. "But I'm pretty sure the heat is affecting me. Because now I can see a beautiful pool of water."

Dec swiveled on one knee and looked over his shoulder. He stilled. "Holy hell, Layne, that's an oasis."

She straightened like she'd been hit with an electric shock. "Don't mess with me, Ward."

"Come on." He helped her up, and with one arm wrapped around her, they stumbled toward it.

He could hear Layne trying to muffle her small moans of pain.

Screw this. He scooped her up into his arms.

"Declan, you can't carry me!"

"Not far to go, Rush. I've carried men three times your size."

She made a grumbling sound but settled in his arms. Soon, they neared the oasis.

Damn. Declan couldn't believe it. This wasn't Dakhla. It was too small, and while he could see date trees, there were no towns, roads, cars, or people.

Layne wiggled to get down and he set her on her feet.

"Where the hell are we?" she murmured. They moved closer, and Layne gasped. "Oh, my God, look!"

The ruins of a giant stone temple were perched right on the edge of the placid pool of water.

***

Layne hurriedly dropped her backpack and kicked her boots off, and then splashed into the water fully clothed. It was cool, but not very deep. She fell forward, savoring the water soaking into her clothes and skin.

God, it felt so, so good.

She turned, floating on her back, and watched Declan. He stood at the edge, filling their water bottles and dropping purification tablets into them.

"Declan, get in here."

He set the bottles down, pulled his shirt off and waded in.

Okay, so Layne was exhausted, hot, and tired. But that chest and abdomen...she drank it in greedily. Every perfect ridge and lean muscle.

He did a shallow dive into the water and came up beside her, water streaming off his face.

"Has anything ever felt better?" she asked.

"Kissing you."

She splashed him. It turned into a wild battle and when he lunged for her, she jumped up and ran toward the shore.

He snagged her around the waist and lifted her up. "Do you know your shirt is now completely transparent?"

"I'm wearing a tank top underneath."

"I know. But I can still see it sticking to the skin of your collarbones, making me imagine what that smooth, baby-fine skin you have feels like."

Layne felt the lick of desire pooling in her belly.

"But, as much as I'd like to strip all this off you, you've had a rough day." He set her down. "You need more water and something to eat."

Mr. Protector, looking out for her again. She watched him grab up the water bottles and hand one to her. Who protected Declan when everything got to be too much? When those horrible demons chasing him wouldn't leave him alone?

She sat on the carved stone steps leading into the water and watched with great interest as Declan washed his shirt and hung it over a low stone wall to dry. Then it was absolutely no hardship to watch him climb the palm trees and collect dates.

God, all those lean muscles. She watched them flex and bulge. He had a strength that was hard-earned, not just surface gloss collected in a gym. He used those muscles for more than just lifting weights or running on a treadmill.

When he returned, he handed her the dates and sat beside her.

Layne managed to drag her gaze off the man and onto the temple. Her breath caught. It was beautiful. It reminded her of Kom Ombo on the banks of the Nile. An elegant design of columns, courts, and halls perched by water.

A few of this temple's columns were still intact. God, she was itching to see inside.

She glanced at the horizon. The sun was setting, and, thankfully, that also meant the temperature was dropping.

"We'll spend the night here and rest up," Declan said.

"I want to—"

"See inside the temple."

"How did you know?"

He smiled. "I'm getting to know you pretty well by now, Rush." He stood and held out a hand to help her up.

They fished flashlights from their packs, and Layne also grabbed her copy of the translation of the scroll, stuffing it in her pocket. They walked up the steps.

"It's beautiful," she said. "I have no idea where this oasis is exactly, but I've never heard of this place and it looks pretty undisturbed."

"An awesome accidental discovery." He shone his light up at the carved pillars. "I've provided security for lots of expeditions around the world that came up empty-handed. They would have wet themselves to discover something like this."

They moved deeper inside. The back wall was covered in hieroglyphs and images. People making offerings to the gods. She took it all in and stopped beside the carving of a woman who had a strange basket headdress and had a set-animal sitting by her feet.

Wonder filling her, Layne read the glyphs. "No one has seen these for thousands of years, Declan. God, you have to be impressed by that."

"Maybe."

She glanced over and saw he was watching her, not the glyphs. "This is a temple dedicated to

Nephthys. She was the sister of Isis, and known as the Lady of the Temple Enclosure. She was associated with priestesses."

"And?" he prompted.

"She was Seth's wife."

He froze. "You're telling me this is an undiscovered temple dedicated to Seth's wife."

She couldn't quite believe it. "Yes."

"The House of Seth's beloved. So, we're on the path to Zerzura?"

"Maybe." She ran her hands over the engravings, wondering if the priest buried back at the dig had been one of the people who'd carved these. She murmured to herself as she translated.

A warm hand touched the back of her neck. "I'm going to find us something to eat for dinner and then set up camp. We both need some rest."

She nodded. "I can help."

He smiled and squeezed the back of her neck. "Stay. Something tells me this will rejuvenate you more than a nap."

"Looks like you *are* starting to know me well."

His gaze dropped to her lips. "Yeah, I guess I am, Rush."

She watched him walk away. There was a good man buried under his dangerous exterior. A protector, a man driven to take care of others. One who quite simply took her breath away.

They'd almost died in the desert. She knew she wouldn't have lasted much longer, and even Declan with his training and survival skills couldn't have held out too long.

She wanted Declan Ward.

She pressed her palm flat to the warm stone wall and took a deep breath. She'd never been with a man who she'd wanted more than her work.

But Declan gave her the space to do what she needed, hell, he'd even been helping her do it. He respected her need to do her job well and that made her want him even more.

Layne realized she was staring at the wall of hieroglyphs like a moony-eyed teenager. She shook her head, smiling, then her gaze fell on a familiar glyph.

Zerzura.

Heart beating hard, she pulled out her translation of the scroll from her pocket. "Find your way to the desert in the west, to the House of Seth's beloved, then the place of the small birds, where he is king."

She looked up at the carving on the temple wall.

"Follow the path of the birds to Zerzura directly into the setting sun. Find the buried marks of the birds and reach the home of Seth and his followers."

So to find Zerzura, you had to head west and find these marks of the birds. Adrenaline winged through her. She jogged out of the temple and down the steps toward the water.

Where she pulled up short.

Declan was standing thigh-deep in the center of the water.

Completely naked.

Her brain took a second to notice the small fire

nearby, with some small animal roasting over it. But all her attention was on the man scooping up water and letting it spill down his hard, toned body.

He didn't have an ounce of fat. She let her gaze run up the strong lines of his legs. He was side-on to her, so she got the view of one toned buttock and the hint of his cock. The rest of him was long lines of muscles, with rivulets of water arrowing down his bronze skin.

Layne couldn't ever remember wanting anything quite this much. God, her hands were shaking.

She dropped her flashlight and unbuttoned her shirt. It took her seconds to shuck off her trousers, tank and underwear. The warm breeze brushed over her naked skin, and she shivered. She was already flushed, her breasts swollen, an empty ache between her legs.

As soon as she stepped into the water, Declan froze and his head whipped up. His gray gaze settled on her and he seemed to still even more. Like a predator sensing prey entering his range.

For a second, Layne wondered if the priestesses of Nephthys had done this. Stepped naked into the water in worship, a sacrifice to their goddess.

Right now, Layne knew this was no sacrifice.

She strode through the water and that seemed to trigger something in Declan. He surged toward her, the water splashing around his feet.

She wasn't sure who closed the last few feet between them. She leaped at him and he dragged her into his arms. Layne wrapped her legs around his waist, and then his mouth slammed down on hers.

God. That taste. She kissed him back, her hands fisting in his hair.

He groaned, his kiss deepening. His hands clamped under her butt and he strode toward the shore.

Layne was too busy kissing him to worry where he was taking her. When he knelt and lay her down, she realized he'd made a bed for them just inside the temple, not far from the fire outside. He'd laid down palm fronds and covered them with their clothes and a blanket from his pack.

She reached her arms above her head and watched as he knelt above her.

The temple columns rose up against the magnificent backdrop of the bright stars in the night sky.

But none of that compared to the molten desire in Declan's eyes and his hard body, inches from hers.

He kissed her again, then his mouth traveled downward, tracing along her jaw, then he nipped at her neck. She arched into him with a small cry.

"Damn, I feel like I've wanted you forever," he rasped against her skin.

Next, he lapped at one of her nipples before sucking it into his mouth.

"Declan!" She tugged on his hair.

"Wish we had more light." He sucked on her nipple before his mouth traveled over to her other breast. "I'd like to see all this smooth skin of yours.

Trace the veins beneath with my tongue."

"You're doing fine," she gasped out. As his mouth abandoned her breast, sliding down her belly, she sucked in a breath. "Don't stop."

"I won't." He lapped at her skin. "Not until I've fucked you so hard you'll feel me tomorrow."

He pushed her thighs apart and Layne felt all her muscles trembling. He made a hungry sound and she felt the warmth of his breath over the most intimate part of her.

"You want my mouth on you, Rush?"

She lifted her hips up to him in answer.

His fingers bit into her thighs. "Do you want my tongue inside you?"

"Declan."

"Give me the words, sweetheart. Tell me you want me."

"Yes. Yes! I want your mouth on me. Please."

With a growl, he leaned down and lifted her to his mouth. His tongue slid deep inside her, pumping against her, licking, lapping.

"Oh..." Layne heard her cry echo around them.

He was relentless, and the sensations crashing over her made it hard to breathe.

Then he moved and his clever tongue circled her clit.

"Yes." She grabbed his hair, trying to move him where she needed him.

"Say it," he growled.

"Suck my clit, Declan."

His mouth closed around her slick nub.

God. She thrashed as he sucked and licked at her.

The sensations were so strong she could barely hold on. Then with one more wild, primal suck, she fell over the edge and screamed her release.

She lay there, panting, her gaze moving upward.

Declan knelt above her, a stark, hungry look on his face. His large, thick cock jutted upward toward his six-pack abs.

Layne shivered again and knew the pleasure wasn't over.

It was only beginning.

***

Declan felt the rush of blood pumping through his body and the sweet taste of Layne on his lips.

Blind need made his gut clench hard, and his only thought was to lodge himself deep inside her warm, willing body.

He needed to be inside her.

He gripped his cock and leaned down, he rubbed the head against her damp warmth. She made a small sound that enflamed him.

"Declan, please. I need you." She curled her legs around his waist, one foot pressing against his ass, urging him on.

He fought for some control. "Shit, Layne, I don't have any condoms." He dragged in a breath. "I'm clean as of my last check up."

She undulated against him. "I get a birth control shot, and I've got no health issues."

"Thank God." Dec gripped her hips and pulled her toward him. At the same time, he thrust inside her, burying himself to the root.

The sound that erupted from her throat was a deep, raw sound of pleasure.

God, she was wet and tight. Perfect. He started thrusting, unable to find his usual control. He was a strong man, one used to violence, and he tried never to bring any of that to the bedroom.

But here, under the stars, lost in the desert with a woman who left him feeling so dangerously close to the edge, he couldn't find that control.

He needed her. All of her. No boundaries.

His rhythm was hard and fast, her snug body driving him beyond pleasure. He was grunting as he shoved himself inside her and she was making small cries, her arms and legs tight around him.

"Touch yourself," he murmured. "I want to watch your face when you come."

She slid a hand down to where his cock speared into her. He groaned, loving her easy sensuality, loving the feel of her fingers slipping between his slick cock and her swollen lips.

Then she found her clit, her sexy body shifting as she stroked herself.

"That's it." He kept up his steady, hard thrusts. He felt her muscles contracting around him and knew she was close.

Fuck. He was close, too. He felt his balls drawing up, the primal sensations growing low within him.

She shattered. She arched beneath him, a

beautiful, stunning sight. He thrust once more and held himself deep. He felt his release erupt out of him, spilling inside her.

"Layne." He groaned her name holding himself still as pure pleasure filled him.

"I'm here, Declan."

As he collapsed on top of her, he felt her arms wrap around him. For the first time in a long time, he wasn't alone, lost in the darkness that prowled inside him.

For the first time in forever, he just felt like himself.

Chapter Eleven

Dec lay in the blankets, staring up at the sky. Layne was pressed against him, her hand idly stroking his chest. He was only just coming down and he felt damn good.

Hell, this was the last thing he'd expected when he'd flown to Egypt.

Her hand stroked lower, over his abdomen and when it met the thick ridge of scar, he tensed.

Her strokes didn't falter, she caressed it the same way she'd touched the rest of his skin.

The black memories, that fucking dark thing inside him, reared its head. He grabbed her wrist.

"It's a part of you, Declan."

"Don't turn shrink on me now that we've fucked."

She stiffened and Dec closed his eyes and released her hand. *Dammit*. He hadn't meant to hurt her or to ruin this moment between them. He waited for her to get up and walk away.

Her hand started stroking his scar again. "It must have hurt."

"You're going to let me off being a dick?"

"Take the free pass. I won't always let you get

away with it. To make it up to me, you can tell me how it happened."

"It was right after Anders... I got hit during a firefight."

He hadn't been as careful. He'd been raw and angry, and hadn't cared anymore if he lived or died.

He'd lost what had made him a good soldier, and the Navy had been right to make him leave before he'd killed himself or anyone else.

But that dark thing still prowled, waiting to drag him under.

She stroked him. "Shh. It's just you and me here."

"The guilt's always there, Layne. It won't ever go away."

She sat up, leaning over him. She pressed a kiss to his scar, so impossibly gentle. Then she looked him in the eye. "No, it won't. But until you look it in the eye, it'll continue to rule you." She leaned down again, her tongue lapping at his nipple.

Dec swallowed a groan, wondered how, with just a few simple touches, she could flay him wide open.

"I see you, Declan Ward. All of you."

He slid a hand in her tangled hair and tugged her up. "No, you don't. The things I've done—" The darkness broke loose.

Declan surged upward. As he grabbed her, a part of him liked her shocked gasp. He spun her, pushing her down on her hands and knees.

He shaped a hand over the globes of her ass. "I'll show you what you don't know."

She pushed back against him. "I've seen you.

You'd never hurt anyone, Declan. You'd never hurt me."

He growled and pressed a palm to her lower back. With the other, he stroked his already hard cock.

He gave her no warning. Just pressed forward and roughly thrust inside her.

She cried out, her entire body shuddering.

Declan pulled out, until just the head of his cock rested inside her. God, what had he done?

Then she shoved back, taking him back inside her. "You fill me up, Declan. So hard, so good."

His nostrils flared and the last of his restraint collapsed. He gripped her hips and hammered into her.

She was warm and tight around him, the little noises she made in her throat said she was enjoying herself. But it didn't feel right. He couldn't see the emotions flitting across her face. Missed the connection he'd felt before.

He pulled out of her, and stopped, his breath heaving in and out.

She swiveled, her gaze tracing his face. Whatever she saw there made her features soften.

"Layne—"

"Shh." She pressed her palms to his chest and pushed him backward. He went, lying back in their little makeshift bed.

When she climbed on top and straddled him, he gripped her thighs.

"Stop thinking," she murmured as she lifted her hips.

When she sank down, his cock slid snugly into her slick warmth.

"Hell." He felt every muscle in his body strain.

She rose up, finding a lazy pace. "You deserve pleasure, Declan. Everybody does. Whatever we've done, whatever we've been forced to do, it doesn't define us. It doesn't mean we can't change. Now, just feel."

She pressed her hands to his shoulders and started riding him in earnest. Now he could see the pleasure on her face, the flush in her cheeks. The starlight turned her skin a pearlescent white.

He'd never seen anything more beautiful. He had fanciful thoughts of priestesses saving the souls of lost warriors. It sure as hell felt like Layne was saving him. Here with her, there was no darkness, no pain.

Just pleasure, heat, and warmth.

She slowed her movements, riding him slowly now. Her green-gold gaze collided with his, held.

When she came, he followed a second later, never looking away from her eyes.

***

Layne woke up with a start, a hand pressed over her mouth. It was very early morning, the light murky. She jerked upright, but immediately knew it was Declan's hard body wrapped around her.

Serious gray eyes met hers and he held up his fingers to his mouth.

When she nodded, he moved his hand. "We have

company." His voice was a whisper.

She heard it now. Voices in the distance, the hum of an engine.

"Get dressed."

As she pulled on her clothes, Declan shoved things into their packs with methodical movements. As their little bed was destroyed, her heart gave a tiny pang.

Declan shoved her backpack at her and she swung it onto her shoulders. "Come on. We need to move. If they spot the fire, they'll know it was fresh."

"Maybe it's strangers. They could help us—"

He just shook his head. She nodded again, and followed him as he crept through the temple. They reached the back entrance and paused. Down at the other end of the oasis, she saw a battered, dusty jeep with its lights on. It illuminated four men standing in front of it. She saw the single tall form, and instantly knew it was Anders.

Then she saw Aaron Stiller beside him. The poor archeologist was hunched over, radiating fear, pain, and exhaustion.

"Come on." Declan urged her in the opposite direction. "Move quickly and quietly."

Layne focused on following Declan, putting her boots right in the same place he did. When the ground got sandy, he urged her on and then took up the rear. As he stooped down, she realized he was covering their tracks.

She rounded the crumbling ruins of what must have once been a dwelling of some sort, and slammed into someone. She gasped.

The man's eyes widened and he opened his mouth to yell.

Layne kicked him. Her boot landed between his legs and he grunted. Declan pushed past her.

He grabbed the man and swung him around. The guy tried to swing a punch, but a second later, Declan slammed the man's head against the stone ruins, and the guy fell into a heap on the ground, out cold.

"Move it," Declan said.

She ran now. God, if Anders caught them, they'd be dead.

Soon, they were out of the oasis and back in the desert.

Layne's chest tightened. Okay, she could admit to the flash of fear. The desert had almost killed them yesterday. The oasis had been their little sanctuary.

Now, they were back at the mercy of the sands.

No. She straightened. Anders was behind them and they were armed with fresh water. And most of all, knowledge.

They had the directions to Zerzura.

"I don't know how it happened, but we aren't near Dakhla, right?" she asked.

Declan scowled. "No."

"I forgot to tell you earlier... In the temple, I found the next clue to Zerzura. West. We need to head directly west and look for special markers."

He stared at her for a second. "You think we should head to Zerzura?"

She tightened the straps on her backpack. "Do you have a better plan? Maybe we should wander aimlessly in the desert, instead?"

"Smart ass." He tugged on her ponytail. "Fine." He looked at his watch. "We'll head west."

They headed off, but Layne took one last glance behind them.

The sun was rising directly opposite, giving the oasis a hazy flush of color. The temple looked beautiful in the morning light.

I'm coming back to study you. Layne made the silent vow. *To show your beauty and secrets to the world.*

Then she saw the silhouettes moving through the oasis.

Declan grabbed her arm and pulled her away.

They moved quickly at first, but once the sun started to rise and the sweat started beading on their faces, they slowed down.

The hours passed, and soon Layne felt weariness tugging on her. God, what if she got Declan killed out here?

"Follow the path of the birds, look for the buried marks of the birds." Frustration welled inside her. "There are no birds out here! It's a desert."

"The climate was different thousands of years ago, right? Maybe there used to be birds."

She huffed out a breath and swiped her arm across her forehead. "Then there's nothing to find. How are we supposed to find buried marks?"

"Come on, Rush. You're not going all negative on me, are you?"

"You're chipper."

He smiled at her. "Sweetheart, I spent most of the night with my cock lodged inside you. Not even Anders, or being lost in the desert again, can ruin my mood today."

A reluctant smile tugged at Layne's lips. God, it was so nice to see him so happy and...lighter.

"Oh, yeah," she said. "Hmm, some of last night is coming back to me...but it's a bit fuzzy."

"Fuzzy?" Declan snatched her into his arms.

She gasped, and while her mouth was open, he took advantage. His mouth hit hers, his tongue delving inside.

"Mmm." She gripped his hair and kissed him back. God, she loved that wild edge beneath the tough, controlled man.

He set her back on her feet. "Remember now?"

She licked her lips, liked the way his gaze zeroed in on the movement. "Yes. Every glorious detail."

He grabbed her chin, his thumb rubbing her jawbone. "Remember, we're heading to that beach after this."

She smiled. "Red bikini."

"Screw the bikini. I'm finding a private beach where I can keep you naked the entire time and push you down and fuck you whenever I like."

Layne shivered. In all her previous relationships, no one had ever talked dirty to her. She liked it.

Declan gave her a light swat on the butt. "Come on. Let's find your undiscovered oasis so we can get to the beach."

They trudged on. Layne searched the desert sands for any signs that Seth's followers might have left behind. Nothing.

"You think the others are okay?" she asked.

"Yep." There was absolute firmness in Declan's voice. "Logan is far too tough and cranky to die. And Morgan and Hale are damn good at their jobs."

"And Aaron?"

Declan's jaw tightened. "We'll get him out of there."

Another hour passed, the sun reaching its zenith, beating mercilessly down on them.

"Rest," Declan ordered.

She flopped in the sand and pulled out her water. The lukewarm fluid still felt beautiful on her dry throat. "There's nothing here, Declan. Whatever signs Seth's followers left, the desert has reclaimed them."

A hand settled on her neck, rubbing. "You're sure?"

She nodded. "I don't want to risk our lives on this."

"Our best bet is to get back to the temple oasis, then. And hopefully avoid Anders and his men."

She nodded glumly.

They drank in silence. Then Layne saw a flutter of movement.

She narrowed her gaze and realized it was just the breeze whipping some sand into the air.

She sighed. She'd started to believe that somehow Zerzura, a haven for the god Seth's followers, was out here, somewhere.

But if it was, the path to it was now long buried.

Another flutter of movement. Layne looked up.

A tiny bird landed on the sand in front of her.

It hopped a little, then took to the air again. She watched, stunned. "Where the hell did you come from, little guy?"

He wasn't pretty. He had black feathers, short legs, and a short beak.

Layne scrambled to her feet. "He doesn't look like a desert bird." She scanned the rocky dunes around them. "How could he survive out here?"

"He's landed again," Declan said.

They hurried over. The small bird was clinging to some rocks.

And right below him, partially covered by sand, was an engraving.

"Oh, my God." Layne dropped to her knees, heedless of the hot sand burning through her clothes and brushed the sand away from the rock.

There, perfectly carved into the rock, was a set-animal and a bird image that looked like their small visitor.

With a trembling hand, she stroked the carving, made so long ago, hidden out here and undiscovered for thousands of years.

"He's on the move again," Declan said.

They jogged through the sand, following the small bird. Every time they lost him, her heart turned heavy in her chest. Then the bird would pop up again. He seemed to like gliding through the air with his dark wings.

"Look, Rush."

Another bird. She sucked in a breath. There were two of them now, both with dark plumage, gliding past each other. "There! Another marker."

It was the same glyphs—Seth's animal and the bird.

"Wait. I remembered something about Nephthys. She was also considered goddess of the air, and sometimes took the form of a bird."

"So these markers represent Seth and his wife?"

She nodded. As they headed down a shallow dune, she realized the ground here was turning much rockier. The dark-brown rocks were like scars in the golden sand.

She found another marker partly buried in the sand at the base of some rocks. They kept following the birds as they dipped and glided gracefully through the air.

When she spotted them again, they'd landed on a larger outcropping of rocks.

As they hurried closer, she gasped. "Look at the rocks, Declan."

"I'll be damned."

What looked like just a jumble of natural rocks from a distance, was actually the crumbling ruins of a carving.

It was twice as tall as Declan and badly weathered.

"Seth," she murmured. "It's Seth."

The figure was seated and definitely had the distinctive head of a canine.

"Zerzura is getting close, Rush." Declan scanned around them.

Layne ran her fingers over the hieroglyphs at the base of the statue. God, her hands were shaking. She concentrated on translating them.

Declan crouched beside her. "So, what's next?"

She finished reading the text and blinked. She felt her heart sinking to her toes. "It can't be." She read them again, looking for any errors she'd made. "No."

Declan's hand settled on her shoulder. "Rush?"

"Nothing's next." She looked up, pulling air into her tight chest. "The text here says *this* is Zerzura."

Chapter Twelve

Dec watched Layne as she sat in the shade of the rocks, staring off into the distance. Her knees were drawn up to her chest.

He took his time working back to her, checking around the rocks. Most were natural, a few were what he guessed might be the ruins of something.

If this had once been a great, treasure-filled oasis, he couldn't see it.

He headed over to her. God, it killed him to see her so upset, so dejected. It wasn't like the Layne he'd gotten to know.

She didn't look up. "It's stupid to follow maps. Even stupider to believe in fairytales. I know better."

"Rush—"

She shook her head violently. "No, I know how life is. Loved ones die, people betray you, terrible things happen. Life is full of disappointments, that's just the way it goes."

He knelt behind her and wrapped his arms around her. She was stiff and tense. "Sweetheart, you know there's good out there as well."

"You don't really believe that."

Shit. Was she right? Had he been so twisted up in the darkness of his past that he'd stopped seeing, hell, stopped looking for the good? Did his friends look at him and see what he saw now in Layne?

It had taken one bright, smart woman to burst through the gloom and show him the light.

"Don't give up." He rubbed his chin on the top of her head. "It's not you." He spun her and forced her to meet his gaze. "These last few days, Layne, you've made me believe that there is more."

Her face softened, even though her eyes were still drowning in disappointment.

"Oh, Declan, and being with you, it's made me realize that I've been letting my headstrong drive to pursue my career stop me from really connecting with people." She touched his face. "Maybe I've been scared to feel too deeply for anyone since I lost my parents."

"Come on." He tugged her up. "Let's take a final look around. A stubborn archeologist I know has taught me to take a bit more time to look for the good in things."

"Fine. But then we really need to make a plan on how to get out of here."

They wandered through the rocks again and both ended up at the base of the god's statue.

"He got a pretty raw deal," Dec said.

"He did," Layne agreed. "A protector who was then blamed for evil that wasn't his doing."

Dec turned and saw her looking at him. "We're talking about a god, not me."

She smiled, then looked up. He saw the birds had reappeared.

"How the hell do you guys live out here?" He had a better view of them now as they circled the statue. "Rush, these guys really look like swiftlets. I saw them recently in the jungle on a job in Asia."

"They can't be jungle birds, Declan."

He shook his head. "They're cave birds. The shorter legs are for clinging to cave walls and the shorter beak is for catching insects. They also have a form of echolocation."

"Like bats?" She scanned around. "I don't see any caves around here."

The birds dipped behind the statue and Dec and Layne followed them.

They were gone.

Dec strode forward, frowning. "Look, there's another set-animal and bird symbol on the ground here."

Layne stepped up beside him.

The ground beneath them dropped an inch.

Dec froze and Layne did the same. Beneath them, the ground rumbled and vibrated.

"What the hell? Rush—?" Dec was reaching for her when the sand and rock beneath his feet crumpled and disappeared.

He fell straight down. He heard Layne scream.

He looked up and saw her falling with him.

They fell downward, rock walls rushing past them. His heart hammered in his chest, the air rushing at his face.

A moment later, Dec splashed into water.

***

Layne hit the water and went under. Water filled her mouth and she kicked. Air. She needed air.

Her head broke the surface and she coughed. The water was fast-flowing, the current strong, and she felt herself being swept along.

"Layne!"

Declan's roar echoed around her. She spotted him, floating down the underground river ahead of her. "Declan! I'm here."

The hole they'd fallen through disappeared as the underground river snaked through a winding tunnel. Damn, the flow was strong, and even if she could fight it, where could she go? The tunnel was wide, the rock walls smooth and striated. She just prayed it didn't get so small that there was no air gap.

"Don't fight the water," he called out. "Keep your head above the surface, and go with it." He was powering through the water, trying to reach her.

She held out her hand. Their fingers brushed, but she couldn't quite reach him. The darkness was growing as they moved deeper into the tunnel.

Her fingers brushed his again.

"Hold on, Rush. Don't panic. We'll have to ride this out to the end."

She swallowed. What if there was no end?

The darkness grew deeper, and soon she couldn't see him anymore. She could barely make out the rock walls rushing past. "Declan?"

"I'm here." Then she heard him curse.

"Declan?"

He didn't answer.

A second later, she felt the water drop away beneath her and she was falling.

An underground waterfall!

Layne screamed. Water filled her mouth and she kicked her arms and legs.

She rammed into the rock wall, pain flaring in her side. But she was still falling, water streaming down over her.

She hit rocks again, and this time, her head slammed into something hard.

She blinked, fighting to stay conscious.

Then the blackness dragged her under and there was nothing.

***

Dec came to flat on his face. His legs were in water but his upper body was resting on sand.

He pushed up onto his hands and knees, coughing up water. What the hell? Had his SEAL team's mission gone bad? Or was he on vacation and had drank too much tequila?

He rolled over and sat, trying to get his bearings. Then his gut cramped. He wasn't on some beach. Above him, a huge cavern rose up, light filtering in from somewhere high above. At the bottom was a large, placid pool of water.

Layne!

It all hit him in a rush. The fall, the underground river, the waterfall. He leaped to his feet, looking around frantically. Where was she?

He splashed along the edge of the pool. For the first time in a long time, he prayed. *Let her be okay.*

He found his waterlogged backpack but there was no sign of anyone else. He kept looking, refusing to give up.

Then he glimpsed a flash of something pale over by the rock wall in the water.

He splashed through the knee-deep water. *No.* She was facedown, hanging in the water. Her scarf was long gone and her dark hair drifted around her like a cloud.

"God, no." He grabbed her, turning her over. She was pale, still.

He hefted her into his arms and charged up the sandy edge. He dropped to his knees and laid her down.

"Layne! Layne, wake up dammit." He pressed a hand to her chest.

She wasn't breathing.

A panic like he'd never known moved through him. "Come on, Rush, don't you dare give up on me."

He pressed his mouth to hers and breathed into her. He kept up the resuscitation, waiting, hoping she'd open her eyes.

He pulled back, dragging in a breath. "Come on! You can't leave me. I can't lose you."

He leaned back down, continuing to breathe for her.

Suddenly, her body spasmed. Dec pulled back

and she started coughing.

Thank God. Panicked relief made him feel lightheaded. He rolled her onto her side, holding her tight as she coughed and water poured out of her.

When she was done, she blinked. "Declan?" she said weakly.

He pulled her into his lap, wrapping his arms around her.

"Hey." She nestled into him, her palm pressing to his chest. Right over his hammering heart.

"You were facedown in the water. Lifeless. God, Layne." His voice cracked.

"Shh. I'm fine." She leaned over and scooped up some of the water from the pool. She rinsed out her mouth. Then she turned back to him and pressed light kisses to his jaw.

"I...God, I was so afraid."

She kept kissing him, along his jaw, his cheeks, his forehead. "I'm fine."

He held her tight and breathed her in. He stroked her wet hair. The rise and fall of her chest against his was the thing that soothed him most. "Let me check you over for any other injuries."

She sat still while he did. She had a lump on her head, but her pupils seemed fine. Battered, bruised, but alive.

Then he felt her go stiff in his arms.

"What?" He pulled back. She was looking over his shoulder.

"Look at the walls, Declan."

He turned and spotted the cave paintings.

"They're prehistoric." She pushed to her feet.

Declan stood beside her, waiting to see if she was steady on her feet. She was limping a little, but her entire focus was on the art covering the rock walls. "Take it easy," he warned.

She waved her hand but didn't even look at him. "I will."

He shook his head with a smile. Nothing could keep his girl down for long.

His girl? He blinked, shocked at the thought. Then she moved, and his focus returned to making sure she was okay.

She walked along the wall. "These are thousands of years old, Declan. Thousands of years *before* Egyptian civilization. Simply stunning."

The figures were simple, but almost elegant in their design. There were images of people and lots of animals. The paint ranged from a deep orange to a very dark red, with a few streaks of white here and there.

He spotted giraffes, elephants, and many beasts he couldn't identify. The humans were just as intriguing. He leaned closer. Some were drawn horizontally, almost as though they were swimming.

"These are all reminiscent of other cave art found close to the border with Libya." Her gaze traced along them, her face alive. "The Cave of Swimmers and the Cave of Beasts are the most well-known. The Cave of Swimmers has always been confounding. Why would people be swimming in the desert?" She glanced over at the large pool of water nearby. "Maybe they were swimming underground?"

"I guess it isn't too surprising," Declan added. "Considering the Great Man-Made River Project."

She spun, frowning. "The what?"

"Libya started a project in the eighties to supply water to parts of the Sahara. Underground, all through this area, is the Nubian Sandstone Aquifer. It's the world's largest known fossil aquifer system. Libya started extracting water from it in the nineties."

"My God." She turned to look at the paintings again. "There was water here all along."

"I'm not sure anyone anticipated this."

They walked deeper into the tunnel and Dec clicked on his flashlight.

"This is just amazing," she said. "But this art is very early. Far earlier than the Egyptians."

"But it must be linked," he said. "It must be a precursor to the Egyptian civilization."

"Probably." Then she frowned. She studied the art on one side of the tunnel, then the other. "Look at this."

Right there on the wall was an entire pack of set-animals.

She studied them more closely. "I don't think these paintings are prehistoric. They are just made to *look* prehistoric." Her face lit up. "I think it's another clue from the Zerzurans."

"Why? Why did this priest of Seth leave these clues to their secret oasis?"

"I think they did it for other followers of Seth

who were looking for a place where they and their god wouldn't be persecuted by the followers of Osiris and Horus."

"So it was kind of like a test, a trial?"

"Exactly." She held one finger up, following the paintings along the wall. "Egyptians liked that kind of thing. The Book of the Dead, and its precursors, listed spells that a dead soul needed to pass through the trials of the underworld. Only the true and honorable could make it through."

"Can the Book of the Dead help us get through these tunnels?" Dec asked.

She shook her head. "I think it was too late in the timeline. I suspect Zerzura has been here a very long time. For now, I think we look for the set-animals in the paintings and see where they lead us."

Dec loved watching her work. She muttered to herself, her gaze narrowed as she studied all the cave paintings.

They started farther into the tunnels. Sometimes the set-animals were obvious, other times, they were hidden amongst other beasts and harder to spot.

Then the artwork changed and turned more colorful.

"They aren't hiding anymore," Layne said. "The artwork here is definitely classic ancient Egyptian."

"Look." Dec nudged her over to the left-hand wall.

"Hieroglyphs. *You who seek Zerzura must be fearless like our Protector Seth and brave Apep's realm.*" She pulled back. "Uh-oh."

"What? Who's Apep?"

"He was the enemy of the sun god, Ra, and also known as the God of Chaos. He attacked Ra's solar boat."

"Why am I getting the feeling you aren't telling me everything?"

"Apep was—" she grimaced "—a giant snake."

Dec groaned. "You're kidding me."

"I'm sure there aren't any giant snakes out here."

Dec made a sound. "The way things have been going, I won't hold my breath."

"Come on, you're the big, bad Navy SEAL."

He mock-glowered at her and they kept moving.

"Seth protected Ra by spearing Apep," she said. "That was Seth's first role in mythology, as a protector."

They reached a place where the tunnel speared off in three different directions. "Which way, Rush?"

She studied the glyphs and paintings. "Right."

The tunnels became a maze. As Layne deciphered and picked the tunnels, Dec hoped they didn't have to get out in a hurry. He pulled out his knife and made a small scratch on the wall.

They kept moving through the never-ending maze.

Layne studied the wall again. "There's the set-animal."

Dec spotted something else. "Layne?"

She spun. "What is it?"

He pointed. "See this scratch? I left it there. Earlier."

"That can't be." Her brow scrunched. "And what do you mean, you left it there? Are you scratching historical cave paintings?"

"Layne, it's not touching the painting. But I left that scratch. We've passed here before."

Her face went pale. "We're going in circles."

Chapter Thirteen

"The key has to be here somewhere." Layne pressed her fingers to the stone wall, careful not to touch the paint.

"Layne. Take a break."

"No, I *have* to find the key. The clue that'll send us in the right direction."

Hands descended on her shoulders, kneaded. "Get some rest, Rush. You're pushing too hard. We've been going in circles for over an hour."

She let him nudge her down and she leaned back against the wall and closed her eyes. "We're so close, Declan."

"Break." He shoved something at her.

She took the nutrition bar and opened it. It tasted pretty bland and chewy. "I'm missing something. The set-animal symbols are there, but they keep leading us in a circle."

"Break, Rush. Switch it off for a bit."

She huffed out a breath. He leaned back against the wall beside her, his legs outstretched. She was caught for a second by the triangle of bronze chest bared at the top of his shirt. God, he'd turned her into a quivering mass of need. She'd never felt like this before.

Declan glanced at his watch. "It's getting late. We'll need to get some rest."

She nodded. "Do you think Anders is following us?"

"Yes."

"Logan and your brother?"

"They'll be looking for us. And I have my tracker." He lifted his wrist.

"The signal will get through the rock and sand?"

His jaw tightened. "They'll find us. Logan isn't the kind who gives up easily. Even when it's a lost cause. He's like a bear—he'll just keep charging. It's his greatest strength and his greatest weakness. And Cal...well, he's never given up on me, ever."

"You love them."

Declan's brows raised. "If you mean in a manly, brotherly kind of way, yeah. I'm close to Cal, and I think of Logan the same way." A tiny smile on his lips. "Logan's saved my ass more times than I can count."

"I assume you've returned the favor."

Another quirk of Declan's lips. "Maybe."

Layne nibbled on her bar. "What if we can't find it?"

"Zerzura?"

She nodded.

"Well, life goes on, Rush. If at first you don't succeed, you work out where you went wrong, and you try again."

"And you keep trying...with Anders. You keep trying to stop him."

"Yeah." A scowl.

She hated seeing that dark look settle over him, the storms boiling in his eyes.

Layne shifted into his lap, settling her knees on either side of his hips.

He lifted his head. "What are you doing?"

She fiddled with the buttons on his shirt, slipping them open. "You told me to take a break."

"So I did." He leaned back, his hands settling on her hips.

"I do like the way you're made, Declan. All lean, hard muscle." She spread his shirt open and ran her hands up his chest. She loved the way her touch made him suck in a breath. Layne leaned forward and kissed him.

"God, Layne." He dragged his mouth from her and pressed his lips to the side of her neck.

She arched back, feeling heat arrowing through her. She ground against him and felt the hard bulge of his cock pressing against where she was hot and achy.

"I want you." His hands started tearing at her tank. He helped her slide it over her head. "I always want you. Can't seem to get enough."

"Good," she panted.

They tore at each other's clothes and moments later, she sank down on his cock.

Declan groaned. "Ride me, Rush. Make me lose my mind."

***

Dec leaned back against the wall, holding Layne in his arms as she slept.

He felt pretty damn good.

He'd dozed through the night and while the rock beneath him wasn't comfy, the woman in his arms felt perfect. He realized now he'd spent a hell of a lot of time avoiding this. He'd avoided relationships and just had one-night stands. He'd rarely spent the entire night with a woman. He'd never cuddled, never stroked a woman's hair, or listened to her breathing.

Hell, he'd never wanted to do any of that before.

Before Layne.

She just burned with life, with passion, and he wanted to feel that every day. Wanted to see her smile, wanted to kiss her every day.

He went rigid. *Oh, no.* He pulled air into his tight chest. He was falling in love with her.

He closed his eyes, felt her heart beating against his and the warm puff of her breath on his chest. He'd gone and done the one thing he thought he was incapable of.

Soon she stirred and lifted her head. "What time is it?"

"Early."

She sat up, pushing her hair back. "Thanks for being my comfy bed." She frowned at him. "Did you get some sleep?"

"A little."

"God, I shouldn't have been lying on you and—"

"Rush." He gripped her chin. "I got some sleep. Now, how about a kiss?"

She touched her tongue to her lip. "We both know if I kiss you, it'll turn into something else, and we'll get naked and have sex."

Amusement hit him. "And your point?"

She waved a hand at him. "You're just too masculine and virile. Stop it."

"I can't stop it." Hell, he wouldn't stop it if he could.

"We need to find this damned lost oasis." Her shoulders sagged, some of the life going out of her eyes. "Or just find a way back to civilization."

"Rush. We're going to find it. You know when I first met you, I thought you were a pain in the ass?"

Her nose wrinkled. "Right back at you, Ward."

He smiled and stroked his thumb down her cheek. "Then I watched you work. Got to know you. Got zinged by that mouth of yours a few times. I realized you weren't what I thought you were."

She smiled now and pressed her hand over his. "And I thought you were a tough, macho, alpha pain in the ass. I'm not sure I was wrong."

He laughed. "But you learned to like it."

Her face turned serious. "Yes. I've learned to like it a lot."

His heart skipped a beat. "Good."

"You aren't going to run off to brood and tell me you're no good, too dark, and I'm better off without you—"

"Shut it." He pressed a slow kiss to her lips.

Her mouth clung to his for a second, then she pushed him away. "Uh-uh, no kissing. That means sex, and I really kind of want that, and then we'll be here for hours. Long pleasurable hours..." Her nose wrinkled. "I can't remember why I'm complaining about this."

"Lost oasis, valuable treasure, bad guy."

She grimaced. "Oh yeah."

"Come on, Rush." He tugged her up. "Time to get back to work."

They scoured the cave paintings again. Went in circles again. He watched her get more frustrated and dejected.

"I can't work it out." She kicked the ground.

"So, you aren't a tomb raider after all," he said, hoping for a smile. "Bummer."

She thrust her hands onto her hips. "My breasts aren't big enough anyway."

He snorted. "Your breasts are perfectly fine."

She laughed. "You did that to make me laugh."

"Maybe."

"We've been following the set-animal symbols, the symbol of Seth and Zerzura, and it just takes us in circles. I don't understand!"

"At least we haven't seen any snakes."

"I guess that's a positive." Then her gaze went unfocused.

"What?" he asked.

"The realm of Apep. We have to pass through it."

"Yeah..."

She hurried over to the wall. "Then maybe I should be looking for symbols of Apep." She moved her hand as she searched the engravings. "There! Look!"

He saw the snake symbol. A glyph of a cobra.

Layne was off like a rocket. She raced along the tunnel and then spun, a smile on her face. She pointed at another snake glyph—this one showing the snake lying down.

Before they took a step, Dec heard something. Frowning, he motioned her to stop. He turned back, facing the tunnel they'd come down.

More sounds.

Voices.

"Shit." Dec nudged her on. "Anders is coming."

Her eyes went wide. They moved into a jog.

Every time she found the snake symbol, she pointed. The sounds behind them faded and soon, the tunnel narrowed. Dec saw they were in a new part of the cave complex.

Now the walls were bare. No paintings, no carvings.

At the end of the tunnel, his flashlight illuminated a huge carving on the wall.

A giant snake with endless coils.

"I think we found it," she whispered. "That's the classic image of Apep."

"Why couldn't it have been a cat?"

"Don't tell me you're afraid of snakes? It'll ruin your macho SEAL image."

"I'm not afraid, but I wouldn't want one as a pet."

She looked at the engraving. "Look at its eye."

He saw the gleam of yellow. "Desert glass?"

"I think so." She reached up and touched it.

There was a grinding sound. Dec snatched her

back and they watched the portion of the wall with the engraving slide back, leaving a black, yawning opening.

Chapter Fourteen

"Well," Layne said. "I think we've found the realm of Apep."

"I'll go first."

"No, I'm the archeologist, so I'll go first."

"I'm the macho former SEAL in charge of your security. That means I go first."

She rolled her eyes. "Have at it, macho man."

She watched him move forward, his broad shoulders almost spanning the entire opening. He moved his flashlight around.

"Tunnel continues," he called back. "No snakes."

She followed close behind, trying to peer around him. She spotted engravings on the wall. "These scenes, they look like the spells from the Book of the Dead, but a little different." God, they were beautiful, the colors still as bright as the day they were painted. "Look, there's Seth spearing Apep."

They kept moving.

"Hold up." Declan held up a hand. "There's a chasm."

She pushed up beside him and gasped.

A small, narrow bridge of rock crossed over a wide, dark opening.

Declan swung the flashlight downward. "Shit."

She hissed out a breath. "At least they aren't giants."

The base of the chasm was filled with writhing snakes. She couldn't make out too many details but she could tell they were different sizes and a few different breeds.

Declan shook his head. "Ready to cross?"

She eyed the narrow walkway. It was barely wide enough for her boot. "Not really."

"I'll go first."

Declan didn't even hesitate to step out onto the bridge. He kept his hands out and his steps steady. There was just calm concentration on his face.

Okay, you can do this, Layne. She pulled in a deep breath and followed him out. It was okay, as long as she didn't look down and didn't move too fast.

Ahead, she saw that Declan had made it to the other side.

Something fell from above and brushed her arm. She paused, her heart thumping. "Declan. Something just fell down from the ceiling."

He frowned, shining his light upward. His eyes widened. "Just keep coming, Rush. Don't look up. Take your time."

"What?" She looked up.

Her stomach rolled. Above, the curved roof was dotted with small ledges.

And the ledges were all covered in snakes. As she watched, one fell down, tumbling into the gorge below.

God. One had *touched* her. She shivered.

"Rush. Look at me."

She swallowed the bile in her throat. If one landed on her...

"Rush!"

Declan's harsh voice snapped her head up. He moved his fingers in a "come here" gesture. "Just look at me and keep moving."

She put one wobbly foot ahead. Then another. Her balance felt off and she felt a burning need to look up.

"Keep coming."

Something flopped on her boot.

She stifled a scream and lifted her foot. The snake slid off...and Layne's balance teetered precariously.

"Foot down," Declan snapped. "Keep coming."

She did and righted herself. She took another step, fighting not to rush. If she ran, she'd lose her balance. She looked down but the space was too shadowed for her to see the nightmare below. She had no trouble imagining it, though.

"Almost there, sweetheart."

Just a few more feet.

A snake landed on her shoulder.

She froze. She felt the damn thing move, heard it hiss.

She whimpered.

"Flick it off," Declan called out. "Keep moving."

Layne shrugged her shoulder, trying not to cry out. She felt the creature slide away.

But she felt frozen. She couldn't move.

Suddenly, trails of light winged through the

dark space. Voices shouted.

"Ah, it is lovely to see you again, Dr. Rush."

Anders' cultured, icy voice made her close her eyes. She heard gunshots and lifted her head. They slammed into the rock wall behind Declan. He was raising his gun and returning fire.

"Rush! Get over here!" he roared.

The thought that he could get shot spurred her into action. She moved steadily and carefully, fighting down the competing feelings inside her body—to run, to scream, to cry.

She stepped off the bridge.

Declan grabbed her arm, his fingers biting into her skin. He yanked her away from the chasm, firing over her shoulder. The echo of the shots was deafening.

He pulled her through an arched doorway and Anders and his men disappeared from their sight.

"You okay?" Declan cupped her cheeks.

"Not really."

He smiled. "You'll do. We need to move. Fast."

They sprinted down the long tunnel. At the end, it speared off into three different tunnels.

"Which way?" he prompted.

"Umm." She was madly reading all the glyphs. "I can't see a set-animal. All the hieroglyphs are just talking about Seth."

Noise and voices echoed from behind them, getting louder.

"Come on, Rush. You can do this."

She sucked in a breath and blocked out the sounds. The hieroglyphs came into focus. "The middle tunnel."

They ran again.

The tunnel ended, opening into a small cavern.

"Careful," Declan said, flashing the light above. "There's a booby trap here. Looks like this spot on the floor triggers a slab of rock to slam down and seal this entrance."

Layne carefully skirted the darker colored patch on the ground. Her heart pounded, and she half expected to see some ruins in the cavern, or more tunnel entrances, something.

There was nothing but a still pool of water.

It was a dead end.

Oh, God. "I must have gotten it wrong. Declan, I'm so sorry—"

"Shh." He was looking around. "We need to hide."

She guessed they could hide in the water, but she'd never be able to hold her breath long enough.

"God, I screwed up."

"Hey." He grabbed her chin. "No giving up, remember?"

She nodded. "If anything happens to us..."

"Rush, that's giving up."

"No, it's not." She remembered the terrible pain of not having the chance to say goodbye to her parents. She hadn't been able to tell them how much she loved them.

It wasn't happening again. Even if the man she was crazy enough to fall for didn't want to hear the words.

"Declan, I want you to know that I'm falling in

love with you."

He went still, his gaze on her face.

She shrugged one shoulder. "I know, you don't want to hear it, and this is really bad timing—"

"Shut it, Rush." The grip on her chin turned to a soft caress. "You love me?"

"Yes." Her lips trembled and she saw something warm in his eyes. "I see past all those defensive 'I'm too bad for everyone' walls you put up."

"God, Rush, I—" He broke off on a curse.

A red wavering dot caught her attention. It was hovering on the center of her chest. She gasped in a breath and raised her head...

Just as Declan slammed into her.

The sound of the gunshot was like thunder in her ears.

She felt Declan's body jerk. She felt him turn and she saw him raise his gun. He fired back down the tunnel.

But not at their assailants.

At the floor.

He triggered the booby trap.

A huge slab of rock slammed down and closed off the tunnel. She heard the horrible sounds of screams as someone got caught.

Then she heard Declan's quiet groan.

"Declan." God, he'd been shot. How bad was it?

He slumped against her and she helped him down to the ground. He'd leaped in front of a bullet for her.

"How bad?" *Please be a flesh wound, please be a flesh wound.*

He sat back, and when she saw the blood over the front of his shirt, her heart stopped. "Declan—"

"Can't...worry about it now. Need to get out of here."

She could hear Anders and his men banging on the other side of the rock slab.

"To where? You're hurt." The enormity of it crashed down on her. He was hurt, and they were stuck far from civilization, with a psychopath on their trail.

Declan needed help and she couldn't get it for him. Anxiety and fear twisted inside her.

"Need you to bandage my stomach. First aid kit is in my backpack," he ground out, sucking in a breath. "Then we go."

She reached over and opened his backpack. She grabbed the small kit and then lifted his T-shirt. The bullet wound was to the side of his stomach. Bright-red blood bloomed. She pressed a wad of gauze onto the wound, hating it when he groaned.

"Wrap it."

She wound the larger bandage around him.

"Help me up."

She slid her arm behind his back and jammed her shoulder under his arm. Awkwardly, they got to their feet.

"Water," he said.

She frowned. "You need a drink? Let me—"

"No. The water, there's a current at the back."

She looked and saw that at the back of the pool, the water was moving.

Like it was draining downward.

"There's an opening under there—" he heaved in a shaky breath "—I think we need to swim."

His usually tan face was pale, and when she looked down, she saw blood had already soaked through her bandage. And he was talking about swimming through caves.

"Declan, we can't—"

"Not going to let fucking Anders touch you."

The fierceness in his voice made her heart clench. Well, she wasn't going to let Anders hurt Declan, either. Not any more than he already had.

"Come on," she said decisively.

They hobbled to the edge of the pool, then waded in. It gradually got deeper and deeper. When the cool water hit his wounds, Declan muttered a curse.

"Hang in there," she said.

"Get my flashlight out," he said. "It's waterproof."

She did as he asked.

"Rush..."

She raised her face and for a second was caught by the emotion on his face. Here was the Declan he kept hidden from everyone else. Her Declan.

He pressed his mouth to hers, the kiss slow and frustratingly short. She vowed it wouldn't be the last one.

What if the underwater tunnel went on too far? She tried not to think about drowning.

He grabbed her hand. "Ready? Go!"

Together, they plunged into the water.

Chapter Fifteen

Dec tried to ignore the pain, but it was bad.

Even swimming through the dark, calm water, he felt the energy flowing out of him.

Get Layne to safety. That was all he could focus on right now. Get her away from Anders and find a way to contact his team.

She was holding his hand in a death grip, and his flashlight gave off the tiniest beam of light in the dark water. The tunnel was wide enough for them to swim side by side.

But they needed to surface soon.

He kept kicking, could feel his lungs start to burn. Beside him, Layne's movements were starting to slow and become uncoordinated.

He kicked harder, wincing at the burn in his gut.

Layne's kicks had slowed to sporadic movements. She was still valiantly trying to go forward, but he knew she'd be fighting not to take a breath.

They weren't going to fucking drown in the middle of the world's largest desert.

He delved deep and found some last well of strength. He kicked hard. Above, he thought he saw a glimmer of light.

Layne went limp.

No, dammit. He kicked, his lungs at the breaking point, his energy gone.

They broke the surface.

He heaved in air and dragged Layne up. She coughed and spluttered, her hair plastered to her head.

A few steps and he felt the bottom. Together, they stumbled out of the pool.

As they collapsed on the ground, Dec's stomach felt like it was on fire. He was bleeding badly. He pressed the sodden bandage down harder.

He didn't tell Layne that he'd bleed to death within the next hour.

God, to think he'd survived so many battles and missions. To think he'd finally found the one woman who'd broken through his self-imposed misery and made him fall in love...

And he was going to lose it all.

"How's the wound?" She pressed a hand to his shoulder.

"It'll do." He said it with all the strength he could muster. She'd found her parents dead, the last thing he wanted was for her to watch him die. Then he looked over her shoulder and everything in him stilled. "Layne—"

"God, Declan. You hold on. I'm getting you out of here."

"Layne. Behind you. I think we found Zerzura."

A sad smile flittered over her lips. "You think I care about Zerzura right now?"

"I think you've dreamed about it all your life and worked hard to find it—"

"I love you, Declan. And I know that injury is bad."

Yeah, his woman was smart. At least he could give her this last thing. He nudged her around. "Look."

Her face filled with wonder. "Oh, my…"

The cavern was huge and the rock lining it was a bright white. Light filtered down from above, illuminating the city that had been carved into the walls, and the large temple in the center. Flitting through the air were flocks of cave birds.

"Unbelievable," she breathed. "No one found Zerzura because it was underground."

"Come on. Let's take a look."

He kept his arm on her shoulders because he was pretty sure he couldn't hold himself up.

The temple was still in good condition, only one corner of it crumbling.

"So easy to imagine the people who lived here," she murmured, stroking some engravings.

Yeah, it was pretty easy to imagine people living here, making their life here.

They walked up the wide, shallow steps leading into the main temple. Each small step felt like agony to Dec but he fought it down. He was going to see Layne's face when they went inside.

They stepped into the gloom. Huge columns rose on either side of them in a long row. Walking forward, Dec could almost imagine it was the aisle of a church.

Shit. When that thought didn't make him start sweating, he knew Layne was his.

He pressed a hand to his side and saw the blood welling, coating his fingers. It was going to kill her that she couldn't save him.

"Oh, Declan."

He raised his head and the air rushed out of him. "Holy hell."

The front of the temple was filled with treasure.

Gold statues, urns, mounds of jewelry, furniture made of gold. It was all laid out with precision, glowing dully in the light.

"So beautiful. And the historical value..." She shook her head. "This is more than I ever dreamed of."

"You found it, Rush. It'll make your career."

She turned to face him. "You think I care about my career right now?"

He was going to say something, but his left leg failed and he stumbled.

"Dammit." She caught him and kept him upright. When she eased back and saw the blood transferred to her shirt, tears welled in her eyes. "Declan, I'm afraid."

"Listen. We need to find somewhere for you to hide. I'll confront Anders when he arrives."

"Maybe they won't make it through."

"He'll be here soon, Layne. In the chaos, you go. Find a way out. The Zerzurans had to have an easy route to the surface somewhere. Use that clever head of yours and find it."

Her lips trembled. "I'm not leaving you."

Fear spiked. He recognized that stubborn look. "I will not let you die here."

"Your gun got wet—"

He smiled. "Most modern weapons can handle a little water. Now, go."

"I'm not letting you sacrifice yourself!"

"I'm already dead."

His harsh words made her head rear back like he'd slapped her. Her cheeks went white.

He swallowed and lowered his voice. "I'm bleeding out, Rush. I need to be in a hospital in under thirty minutes. Even if you can call in the cavalry, it's too late."

"No." A tear slid down her cheek. "I will not lose someone else I love."

He cupped her cheeks. "I'm so sorry, sweetheart. I so badly wanted more. You made me want that. Now, I want you to live for both of us."

"I...no."

He heard shouts and water splashing. They were coming.

He yanked Layne close, heedless of the pain, and kissed her with everything he had. She kissed him back, the taste of her salty tears on his lips.

"Live." His tone was unyielding. He fumbled and pulled his watch off. "The GPS tracker is in this. Logan and Callum will come. You stay alive until then."

She turned the watch over in her hands.

"Now go. Find a hiding place, and when you get a chance, run."

She looked up at him. "Declan—"

"I know. Me too. Now go."

***

Dec raised his SIG. He heard the men coming.

He'd do what he did best and fight. Give Layne the time to hide and then get away. Pain was a living, breathing monster inside him, and he felt the steady trickle of blood down his stomach, soaking into his clothes. But the thought of Anders getting his hands on Layne shoved all the aches and pain away.

There was no way Anders was touching Declan's woman.

He dragged in a breath to steady himself and leaned against the column. He was feeling lightheaded, but there was nothing wrong with his determination.

The first man came through the temple entrance. Dec took him down with a single shot.

More came, diving for cover. Dec moved now, but still taking his time to aim and shoot.

Gunfire echoed amongst the ancient stones. In a place that had never seen modern weapons. Dec had the fleeting thought that Seth might have been pissed off by it.

A bullet winged close by and Dec flung himself to the ground. As his gut hit rock, the pain was excruciating. He sucked in air, forcing back the urge to be sick.

He got up and shot again.

More guys were coming.

Shit, they were going to overrun him. He couldn't see Anders anywhere. Coward was probably waiting for his men to take Declan out of the picture.

Dec moved along the wall, deep into the shadows. If he could circle around...

A kick hit him in the back and sent him to his knees. His handgun clattered onto the ground. He turned, ready to kick back but then he saw the gun barrel pointed directly between his eyes.

Dec was already surging upward, even knowing he couldn't move faster than the bullet.

Bang.

Dec froze. He watched the man crumple to the ground. Dec turned his head and saw Layne standing there, a pistol in her hand.

"I...I got it off one of the dead bodies. I..." She was swallowing convulsively.

Dec got one foot under himself and gritted his teeth as he stood. Conflicting emotions crashed inside him. Fear that she hadn't gotten out like he'd ordered, anger that she'd put herself in danger and been forced to kill. Dec knew just how that first kill made you feel.

He grabbed her. "You saved my life."

Some of the horror leaked from her face. "Good."

"And you didn't listen."

"I wasn't really feeling that whole thing where you sacrifice yourself for me and die."

He pressed his forehead to hers. "You drive me crazy, Rush."

"Well, isn't this sweet?"

Anders' crisp voice made them turn. Dec dragged Layne closer.

Anders stood, flanked by two men who had their guns trained on Dec.

"Looks like this job's become more than just work for you, Ward."

Dec didn't speak.

Anders smiled. It was cold and mean. "I can understand the charm." His dark eyes flicked to Layne. "Dr. Rush, thank you so much for leading me to Zerzura." He lifted his hands. "Your friend, Dr. Stiller, did the best he could, but I don't think he's quite as talented as you."

"You killed him?"

Anders smile was sharp. "He was alive when I left him in the tunnels. Bleeding, but alive." The man looked around, his gaze flaring as it fell on the treasure. "I very much needed to find this treasure."

"So you could sell it off," she spat.

Anders shrugged. "Not everyone cares about history like you do. To most, it's just old junk. And to others, it's wealth."

Anders' gaze skated over her, and then Dec. "I do believe Declan isn't going to last much longer. That's a lot of blood soaking your clothes, old friend."

"I am not, and never have been, your friend."

"Once, we were."

"When I thought you were a decent person. Before I realized you don't have a soul."

Anders shook his head. "Declan, you still haven't

realized that life is all about what you can get for yourself. Caring about others...it's a weakness and a waste of time."

"What made you like this?" Layne asked, confused. "What made you so dead inside?"

"My mother." Then Anders laughed. "No, my mother was a perfectly boring, good mother, and I had a hard-working, normal father. There's no great childhood horror in my past, no bullies at school, no traumatic death of a loved one." He spread his arms out. "I am what I am."

He was a born psychopath. Dec knew there was no negotiating with him. The man would never see reason.

"You're just fucked up," Dec said. "Born that way. So what happens now?"

"Now, Dr. Rush walks over to me—"

Dec's hands tightened on her. "No."

Anders' smile was downright ugly. "I didn't say it was a choice." He looked at her. "You walk over here, Dr. Rush, and my men won't kill Declan. They'll unload another bullet in his legs and leave him out by the water."

"Then he'll die anyway." She was trembling, but her chin was up, her eyes defiant.

Anders raised his weapon, pointed straight at Dec's chest. "But he won't be as dead as if I shoot him right now through the heart."

She pulled away from Dec.

"No." His hands tightened on her.

"Yes." Her gaze clung to his, so much in her eyes. She let go of his hand.

Anders smiled. "Excellent." He grabbed a handful of her hair and pulled her toward him. She made a small cry.

"We are going to have some fun." He stroked her cheek. "This skin. It will look so beautiful with your blood painting it."

Dec's jaw locked. He couldn't think of a single solution. There was no backup plan. No way to get her away from this sick fuck. He had to stay conscious long enough to see if an opportunity presented itself.

"I think the god Seth would be happy I'm here," Anders said. "I think I'm his kind of guy."

"You don't know anything about him," she said. "Seth was a protector, not a soulless killer. You think his followers built this place because he was mean and evil and cruel?"

Anders' smile soured. "I'm going to enjoy hurting you, Dr. Rush. And I think I might make Declan, here, watch."

She spat at him.

He jerked his head back. "Bitch."

Dec saw a movement behind Anders. Deep in the shadows. He forced himself not to tense or look directly at it. Had Cal and Logan found them?

But the movement was down low. He kept his head pointed at Layne, but his gaze on the shadows.

There.

Another movement and something skulked out of the darkness.

Another movement to the left. Another to the right.

Everything inside Declan went cold.

They looked like giant dogs. Long, sleek, black bodies, that would come as high as his waist. Pointed ears and long, stiff tails that were forked on the ends.

Impossible. His chest was so tight he couldn't breathe. They were *set-animals*.

There was a low, menacing growl. The sound raised the hairs on Dec's arms.

Anders' men startled and Anders spun. He opened his mouth to say something...

But the lead dogs leaped forward, attacking.

Chapter Sixteen

Layne jerked away from Anders and stumbled to the ground. She scrambled forward on her hands and knees.

She could hear the animals' growling and snarling. She heard Anders' men screaming. A gun went off, and the bullet hit the ground near her face, sending rock chips flying up. She cried out, covering her face.

A hand grabbed her arm and a scream built in her throat.

She saw Dec's tense face.

"Declan—"

"Let's go."

They sprinted away, and behind her, she could hear Anders and his men shouting and fighting. She glanced over her shoulder, just in time to see a huge dog jump on top of one of Anders' men, taking him to the ground. Then the creature attacked the man's throat. Blood sprayed.

God.

They sprinted down a row of columns and Declan yanked her to the left.

A huge dog blocked their way.

Her eyes widened. She hadn't gotten a good look at the dogs before, but now she had a clear view.

"Oh, my God, a set-animal."

A mythical beast. It was standing there, watching them intently with dark eyes.

"This way." Declan darted between two columns.

She heard the click of claws on rock and a loud growl. She could still hear screams, but they were weaker now.

Then they cut off. Silence filled the temple.

Declan cursed. They'd reached the back wall and there was no escape. They turned.

Three set-animals were moving in on them.

"Please, we mean no harm." She held out a hand.

"Don't think they speak English, Rush."

She wrinkled her nose. "It's all in the tone of voice."

"You ever had a dog?"

"No. Do you have a better idea?"

"Hell, no."

There was the roar of a gun. The lead dog fell, writhing.

Anders appeared, moving toward them. He was rumpled, his left arm covered in blood and hanging loosely by his side.

"*I* am going to be the one to kill you both, not these bloody dogs." Anders aimed at another creature. "Get lost you, mutt." The dog jumped away, pulling back.

"They'll never let you leave here," Layne said.

"They will if they're dead." Anders raised his gun and pointed it at Layne. "I'm afraid the lovely plans I had for you aren't going to work out, Dr. Rush."

Declan moved like a blur. Before Anders could move his arm more than an inch, Declan leaped over a dog and slammed into the man. They both crashed to the floor.

How Declan was even staying upright amazed her. She watched the men fighting, both of them clearly skilled. When Anders slammed a hard punch into Declan's wound, making him falter, she knew she had to help him.

She stepped forward and a set-animal moved in front of her. It was even larger than the other.

Dammit. She stared at its sharp teeth and intelligent, black eyes. "Please. Help. That man wants to desecrate this place. I want to help." She shook her head. "God, I'm talking to a dog."

She took another step and the creature matched her.

"You know what, just attack me, then. But I am helping the man I love." She marched forward.

The dog looked at her for a second before it sprang into action, heading right toward Anders. It clamped its jaws on the man's ankle. There was a crunch of bone.

Anders roared. The other set-animals closed in on the fighting men as well.

God, Declan would be caught in the mêlée.

Layne moved closer, desperately trying to find a way to help him.

Then the dogs attacked. It was vicious. Anders went down under the weight of the animals.

She scrambled closer, elbowing a dog out of the way, not caring if it attacked. She had to get to Declan.

Anders screamed. Two canines were dragging him away, fighting over him.

She dropped to her knees beside Declan. "Declan."

He tried to push himself up, but slumped back down. His face was pale. "Layne—"

No, no. She touched his face.

"I can't move, sweetheart."

"You don't have to, I'm here." She pulled his head into her lap.

She glanced at Anders and then quickly looked away. It wasn't pretty.

"Layne, when the dogs finish with him…" Declan pulled in a shaky breath "…they'll come after us next. You need to go."

She stroked his cheek. "Not going to happen. Haven't you realized I don't want to be anywhere but by your side?"

"Layne—"

Suddenly, there was silence, except for a quiet gurgle from Anders.

She looked up, and the dogs were all ranged in a line, staring at them. She looked at the lead dog, the one she'd spoken to. It was larger than the others, and those insanely intelligent eyes were focused on her. Her heart hammered in her chest.

Then there was a loud crashing sound above.

Rock rained down on them, and Layne stifled a scream. She shielded Declan with her body. One of the dogs whimpered.

She looked up...and saw four figures in beige fatigues rappelling down on sleek, black lines.

Logan O'Connor was in the lead.

Layne looked back at the dogs. "Go." Her voice was quiet. "Go before they hurt you. Others will come here, but if you disappear, they'll leave you alone."

She knew they couldn't possibly understand her, but the large dog just continued looking at her.

"Thank you," she murmured.

The dog stared for another second, then turned and walked away.

The other dogs followed it, disappearing into the shadows.

Layne watched them move out of sight, goose bumps suddenly covering her arms. Never in a million years would she be able to explain this. Nor would she likely want to even try. She turned her attention back to Declan.

"Looks like the cavalry's arrived," she said.

"Vision's blurry."

She bit down on her trembling lip. Logan was here. They'd help Declan. "Just stay still. Logan and your team are here."

A slight smile flickered on his lips. "Told you they'd...find us."

She smoothed his hair back. "So you did."

"Well, fuck, you've made a mess of yourself." Logan O'Connor loomed over them.

"He's been shot, Logan. In the abdomen."

"Not the first time." But Logan's tone was grim as he took his friend in.

"Bro, you did this job in style. A lost temple, treasures, wild adventure, Anders dead." A man knelt down on the other side of Declan. He smiled at Layne. "A pretty lady."

She was shocked for a second. The man had a smoother, prettier version of Declan's face, but blue eyes. His tone and smile were light, but she could see a deep well of seriousness in his eyes. "You must be Callum."

"Don't flirt with my woman," Declan growled.

Callum went to work, checking Declan's stomach. He hissed in a breath. "Made a mess here."

"Was the bad guys...not me."

"Shh." She smoothed his hair. "Don't talk."

Callum's hands were quick and experienced. She saw the same military experience in him as Declan. He yanked off a small backpack and pulled out a field first aid kit.

The other two members of the team appeared.

"Place is clear. Bad guys are all dead." Hale was holding a deadly looking assault rifle. "Either shot or—" he grimaced "—chewed on."

"Thanks, Hale," Logan said.

"I'll take a look at the tunnels, see if the dogs missed anyone," Hale added.

"My boy, could you not have discovered the temple without getting shot?" The fourth member of the team stepped closer.

Layne's eyes widened. It was an older woman, tiny, barely five feet tall, but with a trim, fit body. Her hair was a sleek shade of gray and she had Declan's gray eyes.

Oh, my God. Layne couldn't believe this was Persephone Ward—world-famous treasure hunter and Declan's mother.

"Hi...Mom."

Persephone knelt beside her son. "You hold on, we'll get you all fixed up."

"Putting fluids in now. He's lost a lot of blood, Mom." Callum slid a needle into Declan's arm.

"He's tough." Persephone's gaze flicked up to Layne. "A pleasure to meet you, young lady."

"Ah...you too."

"Well done on your find, Dr. Rush." The treasure hunter smiled, still stroking her son's hair. "You'll be famous."

"That's not really why I do this job."

Persephone sniffed. "You sound like my husband. Nothing wrong with a bit of fame."

Declan's hand moved in Layne's. "You're safe now," she murmured.

Suddenly, he groaned, his back arching. Then his eyes closed, and he went still. Impossibly still.

Her heart just stopped. "Declan!"

Callum cursed. "Shit, we're losing him."

Layne found herself pushed back, to give the others space. Callum and Logan leaned over Declan, blocking her view. She pressed a fist to her mouth.

"Come on, bro, don't you fucking give up on me now."

Logan touched his ear. "Morgan, we're gonna need the basket for Dec."

Layne couldn't lose him. God, she wished she could touch him, but they didn't need her in the way.

"Ah, there you go. Yeah, open your eyes, Dec."

"Layne. Need Layne."

His words were barely a whisper but she heard, her chest constricting.

"Come on, sweetie." Persephone ushered her forward.

Layne touched his pale cheek. His eyes found hers and he didn't look away.

"I'm here, Declan. You hold on."

He watched her like her gaze was the only thing holding him there.

She leaned down and nuzzled his cheek, her lips at his ear. "Remember, I have that red bikini. I want to wear it for you."

Callum shifted. "Shit, with her touching him, his vitals have evened out a bit." His gaze zeroed in on Layne. "I think my love-phobic brother has taken the plunge."

"Here comes the basket," Hale said.

Layne didn't look away from Declan, but she sensed movement above and knew the rescue basket was being lowered for Declan.

"Layne?" Callum said.

"Yes?" She didn't look away from Declan and kept her hand wrapped tight in his.

"I want you to stay with him. You're helping him. Think you can ride up with the basket to the helicopter?"

She didn't hesitate. "Yes."

"All right, people. Let's do this."

Layne ignored the frenzied movements around her, just watched the man she loved, staring into his eyes, holding him to the life she wanted to share with him.

"You can't die, Declan. You've shown me how to feel again and I want more of that." She pressed her face close to his as the basket rose to the hovering helicopter. "I love you. Please hold on."

***

Callum kept his arm around his mother and fought the urge to pace the bland hospital corridor. They'd made it back to Luxor and the Luxor International Hospital was in a large, modern building with good facilities.

He just hoped to hell it was good enough. Cal let out a sharp breath and stared at his hands. Saw his brother's blood still smudged on them. Dec's heart had stopped in the helo and Cal's resuscitation had been the only thing keeping him alive.

God. Cal worked his jaw. For a second, he was thrown back to a dusty street in Afghanistan, another man who was like a brother to him dying in his arms. Cal could smell the blood, hear Marty's choked noises, and felt the same sense of hopelessness.

"He'll be fine." His mother patted Cal's hand, snapping him back to the present. "He's strong and stubborn."

Cal snorted. "Hell yeah." That was Dec through and through.

Down the hall, Hale and Morgan were pacing. Logan was leaning against the wall. He looked relaxed but Cal felt the tension vibrating off the big man. He was like live explosives and could go off at any second. And when Logan O'Connor lost it, lots of things got broken.

But Cal's gaze drifted to the small form huddled in a plastic chair. She was probably attractive, he'd seen a hint of it during the rescue, but right now she just looked tired, dirty, and afraid.

The way Declan had watched her, like she was his very reason for breathing... It made Cal's chest tight.

A buzzing sound made him look down. His mom pulled her phone out of her pocket. "It's your father." She flicked it open. "Go see Layne. She's hanging on by a thread."

As his mother moved away, Cal dropped down in the chair beside the archeologist. "You okay?"

"It's taking so long." Her lips trembled but Cal watched as she straightened and pulled herself together. "He was so hurt."

"My brother's tough."

She glanced sideways. "He's not a superhero." There was the tiniest snap to her voice.

Cal fought a smile. Good, Dec didn't need a pushover. "No, but he has something worth living for." Cal reached out and tucked her hair behind her ear. He knew without a doubt that this was the woman his brother had chosen. "He'll fight tooth and nail to get back to you."

She gave Cal a watery smile. "He promised to take me to the beach."

"Well, Dec is a man who always keeps his promises. It was annoying when we were kids. He could never let anything go."

"I am so in love with him," she said quietly.

God, his brother had gone and taken the fall. Cal shook his head. It sure as hell wasn't for him, but he liked the idea of his brother having a pretty, smart woman by his side. Going on instinct, Cal pulled her in for a hug. She was stiff at first, then relaxed against him. He got the impression she wasn't used to easy affection.

"Did someone say something about the beach?"

Cal's mom dropped down on Layne's other side and put an arm around the archeologist. He saw Layne blink in surprise.

"I love the beach." Persephone bumped her shoulder against Layne's. "Actually I like those frou-frou drinks with the little umbrellas in them best of all."

A surprised laugh escaped Layne.

"Declan and Callum love the beach too. As does their father."

Cal rolled his eyes. "Mom, I'm pretty sure Dec had a *different* kind of beach vacation planned with

Layne. You know, the private kind."

"I don't care." His mom sniffed. "I'm his mother. He deserves to have his plans disrupted after causing us this worry."

Cal softened. His mother had never been one to cry or show her worry. Growing up, she'd been the one to pick them up when they fell as kids and tell them to try again. Their father had been the one to hug them and kiss any skinned knees. But he could see she was worried now.

Reaching over, he grabbed his mom's hand and then pressed it over Layne's, the three of them joined in their love and concern for Declan.

"Someone say beach?" Logan loomed nearby. "I like the ocean."

"You like something?" Morgan muttered from down the hall. "It's a miracle."

There was a squeak of shoes on the linoleum floor. Cal turned his head and saw a doctor headed their way. A surgeon, by the look of him.

Cal swallowed and saw his mother lift her chin. Layne straightened and her hand clenched on Cal's. He squeezed back.

***

Declan lay on his back, the sun warm on his face.

This was his idea of heaven.

He opened his eyes and stared at the gentle waves lapping at the pristine white sand beach. No, he corrected himself, the beach might be idyllic, but heaven was coming toward him now.

Layne swept out of the waves, her dark hair slicked back, and her toned body looking mouthwateringly fine in her red bikini.

As promised, it was tiny.

She sauntered over to his lounger, grabbed a towel, and wiped down her face and body. She took her time, long sweeps down those slim limbs and toned curves.

Then she sat at his hip. "Hello."

Declan slipped a finger into the side of the bikini bottoms. "Have I told you how much I love this bikini?"

She tilted her head, a smile on her lips. "No, I don't think you have." She pressed her hands to his chest and lowered her voice. "But you've showed your appreciation a few times."

Yes, he had, by slipping the damn thing off her, and putting his mouth, his hands, and his cock all over her.

He tugged her forward and pressed his mouth to hers.

She made a small sound he loved and kissed him back. He felt the slightest twinge in his gut, the only sign left of his healing gunshot wound.

He barely remembered the wild dash from the Western Desert to the hospital in Luxor, and he knew Layne still had nightmares about it. But he'd made it. Thankfully, so had Dr. Stiller. Hale had found the man in the tunnels of Zerzura.

"Get a room," a deep voice growled.

Declan rested his forehead on Layne's and once again wondered how their hot little holiday had turned out like this.

He turned his head and saw Logan, wearing a pair of flowered surfer shorts, stretched out on a lounger a little farther down the beach. Beyond him, in the water, he could see Callum paddle-skiing with Hale and Morgan.

His parents and Darcy were around somewhere, too, no doubt making cocktails.

Layne laughed. The sweet, joyful sound filled his chest.

She was happy. Hell, he was happy.

Her discovery of Zerzura had made headlines all around the world. The university was tripping over itself to offer her whatever she wanted, and everyone was clamoring to interview the beautiful tomb raider who found an undiscovered oasis and defeated the bad guy.

When she stroked his belly, he realized she was touching his new puckered scar. The healing skin was still pink and shiny.

"I'm here, sweetheart," he murmured.

She nodded. "I love you, Declan Ward."

His hands tightened on her. God, every time he heard those words, they never failed to amaze him. Layne had brought him back to life, brought him back to his friends and family, and all the things he'd loved.

Anders was dead, and Dec liked to think those people he'd failed were at peace now.

Like him.

He pulled Layne in for a kiss. "I love you too, Rush. I had no idea that a wild treasure hunt for a lost oasis would be the thing that led me to you."

Her finger stroked down his chest. "I think you have a few more wild adventures in your future, Ward."

He stood and scooped her into his arms. Time to head to their private villa tucked away among the palm trees. He ignored the whoops and whistles of his friends and family. "Oh, I hope so, Rush. I hope so."

I hope you enjoyed Declan and Layne's story!

Treasure Hunter Security continues with *Uncharted*, the story of former Navy SEAL Callum Ward and intrepid photographer Dani Navarro on a steamy jungle adventure. Read on for a preview of the first chapter.

Don't miss out! For updates about new releases, action romance info, free books, and other fun stuff, sign up for my VIP mailing list and get your *free box set* containing three action-packed romances.

Visit here to get started:
www.annahackettbooks.com

FREE BOX SET DOWNLOAD

JOIN THE ACTION-PACKED ADVENTURE!

Formats: Kindle, ePub, PDF

Preview: Uncharted

He edged his hand into a narrow crack in the rock face and readjusted his grip.

Callum Ward shifted his weight and then pulled himself up. Sweat dripped down his face and he pulled in a steady breath, enjoying the pleasant burning sensation in his muscles. Climbing—free of ropes and equipment—was a challenge he enjoyed, along with the adrenaline pumping through his body.

He looked up, his body pressed flat against the warm rock. The Rocky Mountains in spring was one of his favorite places to be.

A world away from the dangers and pressures of the SEAL teams.

Not a SEAL anymore, Ward.

Cal stayed there for a moment, breathing deeply. He glanced down at the ground, several hundred feet below him. Then he looked up. The top wasn't far away. With intense concentration, he picked out his path.

Then he climbed.

He loved the speed and freedom of free soloing. He was alive. He couldn't ever let himself forget that.

Or the fact that so many of his SEAL buddies were not.

A few feet from the top, a harsh ringing sound made him start. One of his hands slipped, and for a second, he felt his body swing away from the rock.

Quickly, he moved back, jamming his hand into a narrow handhold, scraping his knuckles in the process.

With a curse, his heartbeat hammering in his ears, he slipped his hand into his pocket and yanked out his cell phone. He wedged the device between his ear and shoulder.

"What?"

"Cal, where are you?" His sister's voice came through loud and clear. "Lazing the day away at your cabin?" Darcy's voice soured. "I hope you don't have company, right now. There's no time for all those blondes tripping over themselves to get to you."

Cal rolled his eyes and glanced at the magnificent view of the valley below—a sweep of trees and the breathtaking mountains. In the distance, he heard the throb of helicopter rotors. Some rich somebody getting a quick transfer to Vale or a rescue helicopter.

"No blonde. I'm climbing, D. Kind of at a critical moment here."

"We have a job."

His senses sharpened. "Okay. Well, I need to finish the climb, get back to my truck, then lock up the cabin. I can be back in Denver this evening."

"Too long. I sent Declan to get you."

Cal snorted. "You managed to pry him away from his new fiancée?"

"It took a little convincing." Darcy's voice softened.

Yeah, Cal's big bro had certainly fallen hard for his sexy little archeologist. It was a little too sickly-sweet to see. Cal couldn't imagine foregoing the variety of lovely ladies out there for just one—no matter how beautiful, smart, or sexy she was.

Live life to the fullest. That was Cal's motto.

"Look, it'll still take me some time to meet up with Dec—"

"Actually, he's coming to you. He should almost be there."

At that instant, the sound of the helicopter turned to a roar. The helo crested the mountain top above, sending a fine spray of rocks and twigs raining down on Cal. In the clear bubble of the helicopter cockpit, Cal spotted his brother's rugged face.

Cal sighed. Looked like his climb was done. "Yeah. He found me."

"Good. See you soon."

***

An hour later, hair damp from a quick shower, Cal entered the offices of Treasure Hunter Security.

The offices were housed in an old flour mill that Dec and Cal had bought and converted. Dec had outfitted the upper level into his living quarters. Downstairs was all open-plan, with lots of concrete and brick, housing the heart of their business. At one end of the large space, computer screens lined the wall, and high-tech computers sat on sleek desks. That was their sister's domain. Darcy loved anything that involved a keyboard. The other corner was dominated by a pool table and an air hockey table. The furious *thwack* of the pucks told him there was a high-stakes game going on.

"Ward," a deep voice called out. "Come and take over for Morgan. Woman is a fiend at this."

Cal grunted at Logan O'Connor and made his way over to the air hockey table. Logan was big, and with a checked shirt, worn jeans, and shaggy hair, he gave off a wild, mountain-man vibe. His opponent, Morgan Kincaid, was about as opposite to that as you could get. She leaned her long body into the table and shot Logan the finger. The tall, sleek, dark-haired woman wasn't just a fiend at air hockey, she was damned good in the field and in a fight.

She looked Cal's way, her dark hair feathered around her strong face. "Cal."

"Morgan." Cal looked around. "Hale and Ronin?"

"In the field." Morgan strode over to the small fridge in the kitchenette tucked in one corner of the space. She grabbed a soda and popped the top. "Both of them are in DC. Guarding some fancy jewel exhibit for the Smithsonian."

Cal took her end of the hockey table and shot the puck at Logan. "You know I'll beat you too."

"No way, Ward. You're dreaming." Logan slammed it back. "You've never beat me yet."

"That's because you cheat," Cal said.

"Cheat? How the hell can you cheat at air hockey?"

Cal lined up his shot and hit the puck. "I don't know, but you do."

Logan slammed the puck back again with a growl. He shook his head, his shaggy hair brushing his shoulders. "Where the hell is Dec?"

"Well, he dropped me off at my place and then came straight here to meet Layne," Cal answered. "My guess is that he's wrapped around his fiancée."

"He's happy."

Cal lifted his head and studied Logan. Logan was his brother's best friend. The two of them had been together on the same SEAL team, and had saved each other's lives more times than they could count.

"Yeah, he is." Cal was damned happy for his brother. Before Dec had met Layne, he'd carried dark shadows from his time in the Navy. Cal knew what those shadows could do to a man. He'd seen too many friends die, people killed, and bad guys get away. Memories stirred, and he shoved them aside. The shadows could kill you, if you let them.

Dec had gotten out, and Cal had followed not long after. It had taken a bullet for Dec to leave, but for Cal, it had just taken losing his best friend.

"He's in love," Logan added. He made it sound like Dec had caught a disease.

On a security job a few months back, Dec had met Dr. Layne Rush. What was supposed to be a simple archeological dig in the Egyptian desert had turned into a wild and dangerous adventure. Layne and Dec had ended up discovering a lost oasis and falling in love. Now Dec smiled all the time, and snuck his fiancée off to their apartment whenever he could.

Love. Cal had never experienced the emotion, and he was fine with that. "Don't worry, O'Connor, I don't think it's infectious."

Logan grunted.

"The love thing isn't for me." Cal leaned his hip against the air hockey table. "There are too many lovely ladies out there to limit myself to just one."

Logan grunted again. "Like that redhead who was wrapped around you at the bar the other night?"

Cal grinned. "She was...enthusiastic."

"What was her name?"

"She didn't tell me. But we had a great time." They'd gone back to her place, and Cal had left before the sun had come up.

Logan raised a brow. "My prediction...someone is going to make you slow down one day, Ward."

"Nah." Cal liked his life just the way it was. He'd had it serious before. Being a SEAL had meant that every situation was a life or death decision. And every decision could be your last. Treasure Hunter Security suited him just fine. He still got to use his skill set, and he was much less likely to end up dead.

He'd made a vow to a dying friend to live enough for both of them.

"You'll take the fall one day." Logan glanced up,

his gold-brown eyes intense in his rugged face. "Like your brother, you'll be a goner."

Cal shot the man the finger. "Screw you, O'Connor. If you want the whole 'love at first sight' thing so badly, you do it."

Something flickered over the man's face, but before Cal could make sense of it, he heard voices behind them, and footsteps echoing on the polished concrete floor.

Dec, Layne and Darcy had arrived. Dec had one arm slung across the shoulders of his fiancée. Cal guessed he was right in his assessment of what the two had been up to. Layne's attractive face was a little flushed, and his brother looked awfully relaxed and satisfied.

Darcy looked her usual polished self, her high heels clicking on the floor. She was wearing dark slacks and a white shirt that tied up around her neck. Her dark hair swung, shiny and sleek, by her jaw. Darcy might be a hacker extraordinaire, but she always liked to look good doing it.

"We have a job." Darcy's blue-gray eyes leveled on Cal. "Cal, you're going to Cambodia."

Cal groaned. "Why are my jobs never in the Caribbean? Or the Seychelles? Cambodia has jungles, which means mosquitoes."

"So pack some repellent," Dec said, amusement in his deep voice.

Darcy ignored them both. She made her way over to her computers. "We've been hired by the Angkor Archeology Project." She picked up her favorite laser pointer/remote and aimed it at the screen.

An aerial picture of Angkor Wat appeared. The sprawling temple complex was impressive, the central structure rising up from a sea of trees and vegetation. The complex was surrounded by a large moat.

Cal had visited Angkor Wat once before. Not on a job, but while on R and R from his SEAL team. It was a fantastic, interesting place to visit. He wouldn't mind another look at it.

"The AAP is a mixed team of archeologists from around the world, and they are focused on studying the ancient Khmer Empire that flourished from the ninth to thirteenth centuries. The team was responsible for lidar scans that were taken of the area a few years back."

"Lidar?" Logan said.

"Light Detection and Ranging," Darcy answered. "It's a sophisticated scanning technology. The lidar device is mounted on a helicopter that flies over an area, shooting the laser. From it, you get high-resolution maps. The AAP started scanning Angkor Wat, and the scans uncovered amazing detail. Completely undocumented features beneath the forest floor."

The images on the screens changed, showing scans crisscrossed with roads, canals, and earthworks.

"Amazing." Layne stepped forward. "I remember this now. It really helped to expand the knowledge on Khmer construction." She tilted her head.

"There was a lot of hype about a 'lost city' they discovered."

Darcy nodded. "Mahendraparvata. The city was never really lost. Everyone knew where it was, buried under the jungle on Phnom Kulen or Mount Kulen. It's a mountain range not too far away from Angkor." Another image flicked up on the screen. It showed a long silhouette of a mountain. "Phnom Kulen is a sacred mountain, and a few temples have been discovered here and there, but what had been found was mainly just rubble in the jungle. No one really knew the true extent of the city. The scans helped reveal the scale of it, connected the dots, and showed the outlines of things buried beneath the surface."

Cal wandered closer. "So what's so special about this city?"

"Mahendraparvata is the place where King Jayavarman II was crowned as the god king back in the ninth century. It is considered the sacred birthplace of the ancient Khmer Empire."

"So, what do the AAP need from us?" Cal asked.

"The team's recent scans of Phnom Kulen have uncovered some interesting structures." Darcy smiled. "They want security for a jungle expedition to a lost temple."

Cal grinned. "Oh, good. Let me just pack my fedora and bullwhip."

Darcy rolled her eyes at him. "They wouldn't give me details related to these new scans. I'm sure they don't want every amateur treasure hunter or history buff invading. They said they'll provide you with everything you need when you get there. They must have good funding because they're paying well."

"Who are the players?" Dec asked.

"The AAP team is currently staying at a hotel in Siem Reap. That's the main city in the area, and the tourist gateway to the Angkor temples. The team is being led by an English archeologist by the name of Dr. Benjamin Oakley." An unflattering shot of a tall man with a head of gray hair appeared. "He's working with a local archeologist named Dr. Sakada Seng." Another photo appeared showing a young Cambodian man. "Oakley has two more archeologists on the team. An Australian, Dr. Gemma Blake, and a Frenchman Dr. Jean-Luc Laurent." Two more photos appeared beside Dr. Oakley's.

Cal whistled.

Darcy rolled her eyes again.

Dr. Blake was a small, curvy blonde with a wide smile. Laurent looked like he was in his forties, with a long, narrow face and sandy hair.

"The final member of the team is their tech guy. He runs the scanning technology. He's an American by the name of Sam Nath." The picture of a younger man with dark hair, copper skin, and a wide, beaming smile appeared.

"Okay." Cal nodded his head. "So I take this group into the jungle to find a lost temple. I've had worse jobs."

"Oh, there's one extra joining the team as well," Darcy added. "Daniela Navarro."

Layne gasped. "Really? I *love* her work."

Cal frowned. "Another archeologist?"

"You don't know who she is?" Layne shook her head and looked at her fiancé. "You've heard of her, right?"

"Photographer," Dec said.

"That's right." Darcy leaned back against the desk. "She's a world-renowned photographer of ancient sites. She travels the globe, taking pictures of ancient temples, pyramids, and statues. Her photos can go for tens of thousands of dollars."

A picture flashed up. It wasn't of a person; it was of the Abu Simbel temples in Southern Egypt. The photographer had taken the shot early in the morning, the sun just touching the giant statues of Ramses the Great. There was a sense of magic in the shot, a hushed stillness.

It made Cal's chest tighten. Made him think of dreams and possibilities.

"I couldn't find a shot of Navarro." Darcy shrugged. "For a photographer, she doesn't seem to take pictures of herself. But I have to say, her work is fabulous."

Cal knew this would be a straightforward job. Get in, get it done, visit Angkor while he was there, and be back to do some more rock climbing before he knew it. "Well, at least I know our friends at Silk Road won't be interested in the rubble of a temple."

Declan scowled. He and Layne had tangled with the dangerous black market antiquities ring in Egypt. The shadowy organization let nothing get in their way in their rush to steal priceless antiquities.

Darcy nodded. "I don't think those mercenary thieves will bother you. This is a solo job, but if you need more help on the ground, let me know. I'll have Logan on standby."

Logan crossed his arms over his chest. "I hate mosquitos more than Cal."

Everyone ignored him. Dec looked at Cal. "You see any sign of Silk Road, you call us."

Cal nodded and looked back at Darcy. "So when do I leave?"

"Now." His sister handed him a stack of documents. "Enjoy your trip."

***

Click.

Dani moved her camera, lining up the girl's smiling face in the middle of the shot, and pressed the button. *Click.* Then she zoomed out, taking in the landmark behind the girl as well.

Dani loved Angkor Wat. The City of Temples was full of amazing wonders. She lowered the camera for a second. Here, at the base of one of the towers of the main temple, the harmonious feel of the place really stood out.

The unique temple rose up into the sky, and its beauty wasn't diminished by the tourists swarming around it. She knew it was a representation of Mount Meru—the sacred mountain that was home of the gods.

What she loved was that every nook and cranny of the place offered something different—amazing bas-reliefs, or nature insinuating itself back into the ruins, trees growing through the temples. She didn't even mind the tourists. Watching them taking it all in, the range of emotions skittering over their faces, it all made her smile.

That's what Dani liked capturing the most. Not just the old temples and the sense of history, but the feelings they elicited. That's what made her photographs come alive—all the things people were thinking and feeling written on their faces and caught in their movements.

Damn, she loved her job. She smiled. She was grateful every day that she made a very good living from her photography.

She zoomed in on a couple posing for their camera that they'd perched on a rock. Young lovers, she decided, by the way they touched each other. She snapped them as they pulled exaggerated poses. Then the man pulled the woman in for a kiss. Dani took the shot, capturing that most elusive of things—love. That fleeting, mysterious emotion.

She lowered the camera. She gave them six months. Then one of them would be itching to get out. She shoved the cynical thought away. *For now, she'd focus on the love.*

Dani set off down the steps and worked her way through the crowd of people walking slowly through the temple. She wandered to a quieter part of the site, where the crowds thinned, and she could hear the echo of her footsteps on the ancient stones. Here, she could get some good shots. She turned in a circle. Hmm, *here*, the light was just right. She raised her well-used Canon.

But there were plenty of pretty shots of Angkor Wat out there. What she was looking forward to the most was her chance to photograph the ruins of Mahendraparvata. Of finding lost temples amongst the jungle.

She stopped again. This time, she spotted a woman only a few years younger than herself. She was gorgeous. Blonde hair spilled over tanned shoulders. She wasn't model thin, instead she had curves that Dani suspected would bring a man to his knees. She felt a flash of envy. When you were tall, with slim hips and a flat chest, curves were always a distant dream. The woman was smiling as she took in the temple's carvings.

As Dani snapped a few more shots, a handsome man wandered closer and struck up a conversation with the woman. They talked for a bit. Small talk, Dani imagined. The woman laughed.

Dani frowned, even as she continued clicking. The man had player written all over him. He had the look of a man who knew what he looked like, and knew how to use it. Her brother and father had the same look—same handsome face, same insincere smile.

With an annoyed sigh, Dani moved on.

She kept snapping shots. She zoomed in, and this time spotted a middle-aged woman dressed in a short skirt and a low-cut top. This time, Dani was reminded of her mother. Julia Navarro Simmons Hall was on marriage number four, and had always judged her worth by her looks. And the bank account of her current husband.

Dani turned away, looking for a more interesting subject. She avoided her family as much as she could. She refused to let them intrude on the life she'd made for herself.

She zoomed in on a man walking up the main path toward the temple.

Wow. She took a bunch of shots. Handsome, rugged, and sexy. The man had a face made for the camera with enough angles to cast some interesting shadows. Dark hair that was just long enough to fall over his forehead, day-old scruff on his cheeks, and a well-shaped jaw.

Next, she took in the body. He walked with a loose-hipped stride, a man comfortable with himself. He was somewhere over six feet with a muscular physique. A pale-khaki shirt stretched over wide shoulders, and his long legs were tucked into dark-green cargo pants. He didn't look like a man who spent much time in fancy suits or stuffy offices. No, he was well suited to the ruined temple beside him.

She took a few more shots. Suddenly, he glanced her way, a frown on his face.

Dani decided it was time to move on. She focused on a small group walking up the steps of the temple, and decided to head inside.

Inside the enclosure, bright-green grass contrasted with the old stones. The group she'd followed had disappeared, and instead, Dani focused on getting a few up-close shots of the engravings on the wall. Devatas—dancing women in all different poses, elaborate headdresses on their heads. The entire site was a group of enclosures, galleries, and cloisters leading in to the main temple.

She wandered up some steps and into a paved gallery. She paused, taking a deep breath. Here, she could easily imagine the ancient Cambodians walking through on their way to celebrate their gods.

"Hey, stop!"

The young woman's scared voice made Dani frown. She hurried around the corner.

Down a set of steps, she spotted a man playing tug-of-war with a woman's backpack.

The man kept yanking, but the woman held on with grim tenacity.

Suddenly, the man shifted his weight and shoved hard against the woman. She stumbled backward but kept her bag clutched in her hands.

"Hey!" Dani let her camera drop around her neck and hurried down the steps. "Leave her alone."

The man's dark eyes widened. Ignoring Dani, he reached down and gripped the woman's bag again. She cried out and fell onto her hands and knees.

"I said, leave her alone." Dani rushed forward, and slammed a hard kick into the man's side.

He stumbled back with a grunt. He was a couple of inches shorter than Dani's five foot eight, but she didn't dismiss his wiry strength.

When he raised a fist, Dani got mad. She kicked him again and slammed her fist into his belly.

"Stop!"

The deep, masculine voice echoed off the temple walls. Behind her, Dani heard the sound of running feet. The thief's gaze went over her shoulder, and his eyes widened.

He turned and bolted.

Chest heaving, Dani turned. And went still.

Mr. Handsome, rugged, and sexy was sprinting toward her.

Treasure Hunter Security

Undiscovered
Uncharted
Unexplored

MORE ACTION ROMANCE?

**ACTION
ADVENTURE
TREASURE HUNTS
SEXY SCI-FI ROMANCE**

When astro-archeologist and museum curator Dr. Lexa Carter discovers a secret map to a lost old Earth treasure—a priceless Fabergé egg—she's excited at the prospect of a treasure hunt to the dangerous desert planet of Zerzura. What she's not so happy about is being saddled with a bodyguard—the museum's mysterious new head of security, Damon Malik.

After many dangerous years as a galactic spy, Damon Malik just wanted a quiet job where no one tried to kill him. Instead of easy work in a museum full of artifacts, he finds himself on a backwater planet babysitting the most infuriating woman he's ever met.

She thinks he's arrogant. He thinks she's a trouble-magnet. But among the desert sands and ruins, adventure led by a young, brash treasure hunter named Dathan Phoenix, takes a deadly turn. As it becomes clear that someone doesn't want them to find the treasure, Lexa and Damon will have to trust each other just to survive.

Also by Anna Hackett

Treasure Hunter Security
Undiscovered
Uncharted
Unexplored

Hell Squad
Marcus
Cruz
Gabe
Reed
Roth
Noah
Shaw
Holmes

The Anomaly Series
Time Thief
Mind Raider
Soul Stealer
Salvation
Anomaly Series Box Set

The Phoenix Adventures
Among Galactic Ruins
At Star's End
In the Devil's Nebula
On a Rogue Planet

Beneath a Trojan Moon
Beyond Galaxy's Edge
On a Cyborg Planet
Return to Dark Earth
On a Barbarian World
Lost in Barbarian Space

Perma Series
Winter Fusion

The WindKeepers Series
Wind Kissed, Fire Bound
Taken by the South Wind
Tempting the West Wind
Defying the North Wind
Claiming the East Wind

Standalone Titles
Savage Dragon
Hunter's Surrender
One Night with the Wolf

Anthologies
A Galactic Holiday
Moonlight (UK only)
Vampire Hunter (UK only)
Awakening the Dragon (UK Only)

For more information visit AnnaHackettBooks.com

About the Author

I'm a USA Today bestselling author and I'm passionate about *action romance*. I love stories that combine the thrill of falling in love with the excitement of action, danger and adventure. I'm a sucker for that moment when the team is walking in slow motion, shoulder-to-shoulder heading off into battle.

I write about people overcoming unbeatable odds and achieving seemingly impossible goals. I like to believe it's possible for all of us to do the same.

My books are mixture of action, adventure and sexy romance and they're recommended for anyone who enjoys fast-paced stories where the boy wins the girl at the end (or sometimes the girl wins the boy!) For release dates, action romance info, free books, and other fun stuff, sign up for the latest news here:

Website: AnnaHackettBooks.com